THE
DELIVERY MAN

Jon D'Amore

Advice & Legal Stuff

The Delivery Man ISBN: 978-0-9853000-6-7

Jon D'Amore and his writings are represented by Howard Frumes of the law firm Alexander, Lawrence, Frumes & Labowitz LLP.

Cover design and graphics by JT Lindroos –
www.jtlindroos.carbonmade.com

Print layout and formatting by Steven W. Booth, Genius Book Services –
www.GeniusBookServices.com

Back cover photo by Evie Sullivan

Cover art copyrighted © 2018 by Jon D'Amore

Published by JMD
Printed in the USA
The Delivery Man – First Edition

Table of Contents

Acknowledgments

As I hoped to achieve with my last two books, people across North America and countries around the globe have told me I succeeded in my goal… which has always been to bring pleasure, entertainment and a smile to the world. As far as that *other* codicil mentioned on the *Acknowledgements* pages of THE BOSS *ALWAYS* SITS IN THE BACK and DEADFELLAS about my wanting a comfortable, relaxing life for myself…let's just say I can't bitch. I mean, I *can*. But why here on *these* pages? I've discovered my greatest enjoyment is to take the stories that have resided in my heart, mind and computer for years (some for decades) and bring them to life. That people enjoy what I do is humbly the apex of my dream.

Thank you *all*.

The happiness in my life has always been due to my parents, Ann and Carmine '*Rocky*' D'Amore. They often, and without question, allowed me to pursue every creative desire and whim within me. They never held me back, no matter how outrageous or astounding it may have sounded or the results might have been. I love them and they will *always* be in my heart.

Thanks to: Melicent D'Amore (*again*) for…*everything*; Stuart Aion; Jennifer Duke Anstey; Glorie Austern; Bert Baron; Kathi Barry; Morley Bartnoff; Steven Booth; Tony Caputo; Christine Corrado; Phil Couch; Michael D'Amore; Anthony Dragona; Gail '*GB*' Geoia; George & Eileen Herberger; Ray Koonce; Diane Lombardi-Fleming; Brian Mahoney; Stan Morrill; Ted Nicols; Jeremy Oliver; Tony Onorato; Julia Peterson; Les Reasonover; Louise Rittberg; Dick Rosemont; Eileen Saunders; Ron

Scalzo; Bruce Schwartz; Debbie Sparks; Evie Sullivan; Tom Sullivan; James Toma; Lisa Tracy; Phil Walker; Helaine Wohl; Ed Wright…all believers in the dream, and caring friends and relatives for life.

The remaining space on this page is for "industry people" who deserve some ink: The Writers Group of Studio City, for giving me the creative support to believe in myself and my writing, and for inspiring me to bring each and every high point of my creativity to an even *higher* level. And most importantly and sincerely, Howard Frumes, my legal representative and a dedicated believer who stood at my side knowing it would finally happen. He's truly one of the good ones. Trust me on that.

Dedication

Carmine '*Rocky*' D'Amore

December 20, 1925
to
January 30, 1994

"Just remember…
Never let your right hand know what your left hand is doing."

John Lennon

October 9, 1940
to
December 8, 1980

"All I want is some truth. Just gimme some truth."

Preface

The story within this book started in the early 2000's and was one cathartic sonofabitch to create and complete. Having moved to Los Angeles in 1999 to write (and foolishly think I would swiftly sell) the manuscript detailing a slice of my life called THE BOSS *ALWAYS* SITS IN THE BACK, I had the good fortune to meet Ashley Rogers at a Beverly Hills party peppered with screenwriters, directors and producers.

Ashley had recently won the Los Angeles Director's Guild *Best Director* award for the documentary (which she co-wrote) *Keeping The Faith With Morrie*. In addition, the film won the Hollywood Black Film Festival's award for *Top Documentary Film*. She also produced and co-wrote the International Documentary Association's *Highest Achievement Award* nominee, *Black Mesa*, detailing Northern Arizona's Navajo-Hopi land dispute.

After reading the recently-completed 279 pages of THE BOSS, Ashley immediately became a fan. At the time, I didn't know how fortunate I was to have her in my corner. From the start she knew my story and I needed representation. I was then taught that prior to venturing into the murky, cannibalistic, shark-infested waters of managers, agents, producers and publishers, having an experienced attorney was the *only* way to start.

And she was right.

Think about it. Who's going to read and negotiate the contracts you sign *with* those managers, agents, producers and publishers? *You?* Fugedabowdit!

That was why Ashley took me to the Century City office of Howard Frumes, to whom I presented a copy of my hefty manuscript, followed by him presenting me a litany of reasons why I'll "…never get a book like this sold in L.A."

The story of how small and insignificant I felt after that meeting has been told many times in a variety of circles. Yet, the lessons I learned during that 30 minute (or less) meeting will stay with me for a lifetime (and maybe a little longer).

Several days later, Howard personally called me. I assumed it was because of my friendship with Ashley Rogers that he was taking the high road by not having his assistant tell me to pick up the manuscript and that he was going to do it himself.

I was wrong.

Howard had taken my 279 page manuscript home. Fortunately, I included a slick multi-colored cover showing the title and my name in large bold letters over silhouettes of a limousine and a naked woman with a nice pair of dice. In what I still refer to as "A *very* lucky moment for me," he looked at the cover, became intrigued, picked up the manuscript and started reading.

Between the writing and the story itself, he didn't stop. He couldn't stop.

Since then, Howard Frumes has been my literary attorney, source of moral support and a friend. And after the experiences I've had with attorneys, coming from *me*...those words mean something.

Based on my attorney's suggestion, I learned and honed the art of screenwriting (which also allowed me to pay a few bills during my L.A. existence). He then suggested I write five screenplays of various genres, just to see if I could do it. I thought it was a brilliant idea.

At the time, and considering where I resided, I was meeting people whose lives were as interesting as mine (or at least the part I wrote about in THE BOSS), yet I observed a stream of recurring "personal reasons" for their relocation to Southern California...and those "reasons" weren't always the happiest of stories.

They were stories *many* have lived through.

I decided to write one of the screenplays based on those who weren't able to make it through the hard times. The stories within THE DELIVERY MAN, both the screenplay and this book, were written for all those with similar tales and experiences. As I said, it was painfully cathartic to write these accounts and convey them in a way everyone would like to see them told and unfold, while also being entertained.

I wrote three, and co-wrote two, unrelated scripts within four years while working on screenplays for others (to make a few bucks). I had completed my five. Howard was impressed, and our relationship maintained.

Howard's support and knowledge guided me through the releases and tours for THE BOSS *ALWAYS* SITS IN THE BACK, DEADFELLAS, and now THE DELIVERY MAN. More than anything, I'm thankful to him for providing the impetus for me to create and co-create those original screenplays...and I'm *truly* grateful THE DELIVERY MAN was one of them.

Of course, I wouldn't know Howard had it not been for Ashley Rogers, but she knows she has my heartfelt love and the deepest bow of gratitude for being a friend, a fan...and in my life.

It's *all* been a slice.

The names in this story have been made up, *or* they've randomly been taken from my phonebook...but they are *not* intended to be, in any way, conducive to the characters they may portray in this fictional story.

I use ***italics*** and ***ellipses*** (such as: ...). Why? Because *that's the way we speak!* They are there to alter the way you read.

Italics *emphasize* the specific word.

Ellipses are used as a timing rest...while staying on the same subject.

The italics and ellipses will make the reading of this story more enjoyable and bring the characters to life.

As usual, I've included a ***Cast of Characters*** at the end (in order of appearance)...just in case you need to reference it once in a while.

Oh, and if those last six paragraphs sound familiar...check out THE BOSS *ALWAYS* SITS IN THE BACK and DEADFELLAS. Enjoy!

*"To understand the meaning of one story,
you must often know the details of several others."*

Italian Proverb

CHAPTER 1

In Medias Res (*Into The Middle Of Things*)

It was a perfect mid-July Saturday when the rented 2017 dark-blue Chevrolet Impala pulled up to 47 Sunset Lane in Mamaroneck, New York. The driver noticed the perfectly manicured lawn looked like all the other lawns in front of all the *other* expensive homes that lined the streets of the affluent neighborhood.

In the lavish backyard, lined on three sides by twelve foot hedges for privacy, Patti Smith's "Dancing Barefoot" emanated from outdoor speakers tuned to SiriusXM's Retro-80s station.

Tommy, the early-30s play-thing of 47 year old Sherry Hoffman, wore shorts extending below his knees, sandals and a Hawaiian shirt as he stood on the stone patio working the three-tiered barbeque, cooking lobster tails and ears of corn while sucking his nearly empty Bloody Mary through a straw.

Sherry, the owner of a strikingly attractive face thanks to her favorite plastic surgeon, wore sunglasses and a thin summer robe. Holding a fresh Bloody Mary in one hand and a Registered Mail envelope in the other, she strode out of the house onto the patio through the sliding screen door, visibly on a mission to get back to the chaise lounge she was forced to leave in order to sign for the letter.

It was a letter Sherry had long been waiting for.

In spite of her rush, she slowed her pace to admire the flowerbeds filled with lilies of multiple varieties and colors.

Sherry *loved* her lilies.

She placed the drink and envelope on a low wicker table next to the chaise and slipped off her robe, revealing a bikini bottom and two perfectly-sized, well-constructed sun-bronzed breasts...again thanks to her plastic surgeon.

After coating herself in tanning lotion and taking a long swallow of the Bloody Mary, Sherry placed the glass on the table, sat down and eyed her attorney's law firm logo atop the left corner of the envelope, then anxiously opened it.

Reading each page in detail and with great delight, she took another mouthful of the cold drink, sat back and under her breath proudly said, "I got it. I got it...*all*," then her eyes hungrily returned to the paperwork.

As the song faded, Sherry and Tommy heard the doorbell ring through the screen door.

Tommy continued to cook.

Sherry continued to read.

'Til Tuesday's "Voices Carry" began as the doorbell rang again...and again.

"Can you get that, Tommy-honey?" Sherry asked coyly, having no intention of getting up again.

With an annoyed frown on his chiseled face, he turned toward her and called back, "What's it look like I'm doin' here?" then returned his attention to the lobsters, corn and the now-empty Bloody Mary in his hand.

Visibly pissed off, the topless woman rose from the chair, dropped the pages on the cushion and put on her robe. Walking across the grass and behind Tommy's back, she flipped him the finger and accompanied it with an evil look. It was only when she approached the lilies that her demeanor changed as she inhaled their sweet scent and gently touched them.

Tommy was oblivious to her annoyance while he held up his drink and yelled out, "And make some more Bloody Marys before you come back!"

Sherry was already in the house, and though she heard him, she had no intention of responding or making *anything*. That was what *he* was for.

Walking through a kitchen built for a chef and with music coming from the house speakers, Sherry pranced into the elegantly decorated dining and living rooms, each containing two-or-more vases filled with lilies.

The bell rang again as she made her way to the foyer.

The newly divorced woman opened the door to find a delivery man. He was tall, handsome, in his mid-40s, wearing stylish sunglasses, casual clothes and thin black leather gloves. In his left hand was an exquisite arrangement of multi-colored lilies. In spite of his good looks, she paid him no mind as her focus went solely to the flowers.

He smiled and read off a clipboard, "Sherry Hoffman?"

"Yes," she replied, still staring at the arrangement.

As he handed her the flowers she grabbed the small envelope pinned to them, turned away from the door and fondly looked toward the backyard, assuming Tommy had them delivered and *that* was why he didn't want to answer the bell. She pulled the card from the envelope to see nothing written on it.

Confused, she turned inquisitively to the Delivery Man to find she was facing a silencer connected to a 9mm Walther P38.

The woman's expression turned to shock as he put his left index finger to his lips and softy said, "*Shhhhhh.*"

Sherry was frozen. She couldn't move. She couldn't even scream.

In a gentle and calm voice, the Delivery Man said, "You know what you did."

Though unable to speak, her eyes filled with tears.

Emotionless, he continued, "The flowers are from Mark. *This*…is from me."

And with that, he pulled the trigger, putting a hole in the center of her forehead.

Blood sprayed the wall behind Sherry as her body and the lilies fell to the floor.

Stepping inside the doorway, the Delivery Man emptied the semi-automatic's 8 round magazine into her body, then closed the door and walked to the Chevy as the music continued to play.

From the backyard, Tommy looked toward the house and yelled, "Hey Sherry! Don't forget the Bloody Marys!"

A 24 hour bowling alley in Seoul, South Korea wasn't a place many of Ronnie Gladue's friends in Seattle, Washington would expect to find him. They knew he had a thing for young Asian women, but seeing as their population in Seattle alone should have been enough for him to choose from, no one thought he'd actually go to Asia to find them.

But that's where he was.

It was close to midnight on Thursday, August 10th, and except for one worker at the counter and another at the bar, the place was empty. On one of the lanes, Ronnie, 49 years old, five-foot-eight, good looking, with a half-smoked cigarette hanging from his lips and an air of *sleaze* about him, rolled a strike.

Sitting behind him were two cute, short-skirted, barely-20 year old Korean girls surrounded by empty beer bottles and cigarette butt-filled ashtrays. The girls applauded, squealed and giggled at his bowling expertise. Speaking in broken-English, one yelled, "Three in a row!" and the other chimed in, "That's *great*, Ronnie!"

He backed away from the lane, then turned to paw and fondle the breasts of each girl, neither of whom had any problem cuddling up and letting him grab whatever he wanted.

"Can I have another beer, Ronnie?" one asked as her hand reached down to rub his crotch.

"Have whatever you want…it's a party!" he boasted. After taking a swig of beer and a drag on his cigarette, Ronnie said, "I gotta take a leak," then pointed to the ball-return rack, smirked and uttered, "Keep my balls warm while I'm gone."

He gave a stupid laugh and walked away as one of the girls struggled to pick up a ball and bowl…only to have it go into the gutter.

Knowing no one would be in the Men's Room at that time of night, once he entered, Ronnie let out a burp and a fart, both of equal volume and odor, then walked to one of the four urinals, threw what was left of his cigarette into it and began the process of unzipping and getting his dick out to pee.

Wearing thin black leather gloves and carrying a bowling-ball bag, the Delivery Man entered…having to wave away Ronnie's lingering aroma. He calmly looked to see there were no feet beneath the stalls and no one other than Ronnie at the urinals. He quietly flipped the lock on the entrance door, walked to the urinal next to Ronnie and gave a friendly smile.

"How you doin'?" he asked Ronnie.

Ronnie eyed the stranger and arrogantly replied, "You sound pretty far from home, pal," then returned his gaze to the wall in front of him to continue peeing.

"You're Ronald Gladue from Seattle, aren't you?"

Ronnie raised an eyebrow, scowled, stopped peeing and turned to the Delivery Man. With his dick hanging out of his pants, he filled his chest and indignantly asked, "Who the fuck are you?"

Not getting a response and with the intention of kicking the shit out of the intruder, Ronnie looked down to put his dick away and zip up. But when he raised his head and began to ask, "I said who the fuck are--" he was looking at the silencer of the Delivery Man's Walther P38.

Ronnie froze.

The Delivery Man placed the bag on the floor and put his index finger to his lips.

"*Shhhhh.*"

With his free hand, the Delivery Man took a bowling ball from the bag, held it in his palm and said, "Now Ronnie, let's talk about Anita."

Fear overcame Ronnie's face.

"She loved you. She trusted you. Then you took everything that wasn't yours and left the country. Now, she's penniless and a medicated vegetable. So *this*…is from Anita."

The Delivery Man smiled and slid his hand from the bottom of the ball, dropping it squarely onto Ronnie's right foot.

Screaming in pain, Ronnie stiffened and looked at his attacker…afraid to move.

"And *this*…is from me."

A bullet went into Ronnie's forehead, causing blood to spray the tile walls and floor, and the late-night bowler's body to crumple. The magazine was emptied into him, with only the shell casings making noise as they hit the floor.

The shooter put the ball and his weapon in the bag, unlocked the door and stepped out. Before leaving the building, he respectfully nodded and waved to Ronnie's dates.

They smiled, nodded and waved back.

As the Delivery Man put the bowling ball bag onto the rental car's backseat, he looked at the Seoul skyline, reminiscing how much he enjoyed the summer evenings there.

CHAPTER 2

Some Backstory – Charles & Pamela Adams

At 11:37 on the morning of Thursday, April 21ˢᵗ, 2016, in the Allen County Courthouse in Fort Wayne, Indiana, 59 year old Judge Mahoney sat on the bench in front of the state flag. From his high-back chair he looked at the gallery's audience of two dozen, most of them not paying attention to the case going on in the well, the section within the bar where all the action takes place. They had their *own* problems.

Standing at the defendant's table was 41 year old Charles Adams. "Charlie" to all who knew him was the type everyone called "a great guy" and "a real friend." He had always worked hard and was regarded as the most honest person anyone knew, but that morning his face was drawn and his eyes were swollen from crying.

Next to Charlie stood his attorney, a man who would never be accused of being the most intelligent lawyer in the courthouse that day, or *any* day. In addition, he kept shuffling his paperwork whenever the judge spoke... which annoyed Mahoney.

Seated at the plaintiff's table was 33 year old Pamela Adams, slyly grinning and dressed to the hilt. Next to her was the prosecuting attorney, a woman as stylishly attired as her client, and the owner of a firm that dealt solely in divorce law, and only represented female clients.

Sitting in the audience just behind Pamela was Eleanor, a well-endowed and well-dressed woman in her mid-50s. She amorously smiled and winked at Judge Mahoney. Without focusing directly on her, the judge nodded in her direction, grinned, then within a few seconds held up a paper and angrily eyed the defendant.

"Charles Adams, based on the testimony and evidence previously put before this court...you've been charged with and have been found guilty of Domestic Assault."

Life itself seemed to leave Charlie. His face turned white. He struggled to breathe and his legs buckled...though none of it was noticed by his attorney who stared in fear as the judge continued, "I'm making the current Temporary Restraining Order *permanent*. You have five days to remove your possessions from the marital residence under police supervision, with no more than sixty minutes to do so."

Charlie gathered himself the best he could and attempted to say something.

"Your honor--"

His attorney raised a hand to keep Charlie quiet.

Judge Mahoney didn't skip a beat.

"And be advised...if the plaintiff is contacted or confronted by you in *any manner*, you'll spend up to two years in jail for each offense." Raising his voice for effect, he asked, "Do you understand?" then eyed the buxom woman in the front row. She again winked.

"Your honor...I never touched her!" Charlie yelled in terror and confusion.

"Answer the question. Do you understand what I *said?*" repeated the judge.

"*Understand?* How can I understand that you're convicting me of something I didn't do? And based on no evidence! None at *all!*" cried Charlie through tears.

"Counselor!" the judge barked. "You have thirty seconds to advise your client of court procedure or he'll be found in contempt."

Sweat streamed from the defense attorney's forehead because the judge's anger scared the shit out of him. The lawyer turned and got close enough to his client to angrily whisper, "Shut the fuck up or you're gonna get us *both* in trouble. Just tell him you understand and we'll appeal the decision."

Charlie wasn't taking anymore advice. He needed to have his say. With his last bit of strength he pushed the lawyer aside and looked at the judge.

"Your honor...she *lied*. Her *lawyer* lied. They had no *proof*. No *evidence*. You just took their word without *any proof!* How? How can you do that? How can I defend myself against *that?*"

"Take it up in an appeal," the judged growled back, then banged the gavel and yelled, "Bailiff! Secure and remove the defendant."

Pamela, her attorney and the woman behind them openly smiled at the outburst and the results.

Two large court officers rushed toward Charlie. One stood before him while the other roughly handcuffed the limp defendant from behind.

The judge looked down at the emotionally beaten Charlie and said, "Mr. Adams, for your outburst I'm fining you five-hundred dollars and you're going to spend the night in the County jail for contempt…and when you return to my courtroom tomorrow, I'll expect the correct answer to my question." Then the judge banged the gavel and decreed, "This case is adjourned until ten-fifteen tomorrow morning."

With his hands secured and his near lifeless body being supported by the officers, Charlie looked at his inept attorney, then at Judge Mahoney, and with what little energy and volume he had, he repeated, "I didn't *do* anything."

Mahoney slammed the gavel again and yelled, "A *thousand* dollars and *two* nights! Want to make it *three thousand* and a *week?*" then he looked at the bailiffs and barked, "Get him out of here."

In tears, Charlie was shuffled out of the courtroom via a side door as the next case was called. The attorneys packed up their briefcases and everyone involved in "the Adams hearing" left through the large rear doors.

Once the victorious plaintiff and her attorney were in the hall, Eleanor walked up to Pamela and affectionately hugged her. Whispering into Pamela's ear, she said, "See honey, I told you I'd take care of everything. I just needed to sit behind you and he'd know what to do."

They looked eye-to-eye as Pamela said, "Thank you, Aunt Ellie."

Exiting an elevator and striding down the long marble hall walked Rick, 36, handsome and as well dressed as those he approached from behind. Gently touching Pamela's shoulder, she spun around, saw him and dove into his embrace.

As the couple kissed, Pamela's attorney showed no emotion as she hung up her cell-phone and said, "I have to go to my office. I'll send copies of the R.O. once I get them, then we'll issue the divorce papers. He'll be served in two to three days." To her, it was all about business and the buck.

Once the lovers separated their lips and bodies, Pamela blew a kiss to the lawyer who had already turned and walked away.

Aunt Ellie stepped close to her niece, whispered, "And *I* have to go fuck a judge during his lunch break," then leaned back and winked. They exchanged cheek-kisses, then the older woman swayed her ass as she returned to the courtroom. Pamela placed her hands on each side of Rick's head, pulled him to her mouth and exchanged passionate kisses.

Observing it all, in the courtroom and in the hall...was the Delivery Man.

It was a drab afternoon on Monday, April 25th, in Fort Wayne with the rain going from a drizzle to a downpour then back to a drizzle throughout the day.

At the curb of Charles Adams' home was a moving truck with three men sitting in the cab, out of the rain and ready to do their job as soon as Pamela opened the front door to let them in.

Thanks to Judge Mahoney, two large Fort Wayne Police Officers had been assigned to accompany the homeowner. The officers were there to insure Pamela wasn't harassed in any manner during the sixty minutes her husband was allotted to remove every semblance of his life before they married less than four years earlier.

With the police on each side of him, Charlie rang the bell. Shaking his head and holding back tears, he said with a sad laugh, "I never thought I'd have to ring the bell to get into my own house."

The only reaction from the officers was when one looked at his watch and said, "Your hour starts now."

"I'm not *in the house* yet," Charlie bellowed, looking up at a cop who couldn't care less about what was just said. Realizing it was a no-win situation, he rang the bell again.

Hearing approaching steps from inside, Charlie turned and signaled the moving men to come to the front door. The lock turned and the door opened...but when Charlie turned around he wasn't expecting to see Rick in the doorway and wearing a robe.

"Where's Pam? Who are *you?*" asked the confused homeowner.

As the movers stepped behind the others to get out of the rain, Rick looked at the policemen and said, "Hello officers," then glared at Charles. "Charlie, Pam has a Restraining Order against you, so you're not allowed to see her. She said your stuff's in the garage. I'll open the door so you can take it away."

Frustrated, Charlie angrily and loudly asked, "What are you talking about? Who the hell *are* you? I only have an hour to get my things, so let us in. Get out of the way."

Charlie went to push Rick aside, but the officers grabbed his shoulders and pulled him back to where he started.

Rick, again addressing the officers, said, "You can see why Miss Adams doesn't want him in the house. There's nothing of his in here anyway...it's all in the garage." Then the boyfriend looked at the again-beaten-Charles Adams and said, as if berating him, "If you have a problem with that, contact the judge. You have a cell-phone, right? Otherwise, go to the garage and I'll open the door."

The moving men saw the writing on the wall as they walked to the garage and waited in the rain. Charlie stood there, a policeman on each side of him, while Rick shut the door in his face.

A minute later the large 2-car garage door electronically rose, revealing a new Lincoln MKZ on one side, and eight large, overstuffed plastic trash bags on the other.

The door in the rear of the garage opened and Rick entered from the house.

The movers, the policemen and Charlie quickly stepped inside to get out of the rain.

Pointing to the trash bags, Charlie asked, "What are *those?*"

Rick offhandedly responded, "Your clothes."

"You're crazy!" yelled the incessant Charlie. "Where's my stereo? Where's my furniture? My parent's wedding pictures? My books? My jewelry?"

Rick snickered, "Pam said this is all you have. The rest is marital property, and because you've been issued divorce papers, you'll have to deal with it in court as part of the settlement."

Charlie's body-language had the cops ready to react as he yelled louder, "She's *lying!* She's *fucking lying!* Everything in that house was mine *years* before I met her!" The emotionally shot Charlie turned to the cops and with tears running down his face, pleaded, "You've got to get me in the house! My *life*...everything I own is in there!"

As if perfectly timed, Pamela Adams, also in a robe and looking like she spent the day getting happily fucked, entered from the house and walked directly to Rick, who put his arm around her.

It devastated Charlie.

She took her dreamy eyes from her lover, looked coldly at her husband and said, "Unless you have receipts for what's inside, you'll have to *prove* everything's yours. The clothes in those bags are all you have here…and I want them *out*." Then she raised her voice and barked, "*Now!*"

Charlie was in shock. Crushed. In tears.

"How? How can you say that, Pammie? How?"

He took a step toward her…his hands extended as if pleading. The police grabbed his arms, stopping any forward movement.

Pamela acted, and then *over*-acted, as if she was threatened by his step toward her and screamed loud enough for the neighborhood to hear, "Get away from me! Get him out of here! Get that lunatic and his stuff out of *my house!*"

Struggling in the arms of the officers, Charlie looked at Pamela through tears and yelled back, "*Your house? Your house?* She's *lying!*"

The cops easily shuttled the smaller man out of the garage and down the driveway…now with several neighbors watching. As it began to rain harder, one of officers told the movers to put the eight trash bags in the trunk of Charlie's car…and they did.

Then Charles Adams was led to his vehicle and followed by the police until he crossed the border of Allen County.

CHAPTER 3

More Backstory – Steve Meyers & The Evans Girls

In one of the countless malls along Bergen County, New Jersey's Route 17, it was just another Saturday afternoon in early May, 2016, at a TJ Maxx. An early summer had already shown its face, but the insane sale days of Memorial Day Weekend were still a few weeks away.

Attractive brunette, well dressed, 41 year old Ginger Evans was shopping with her pretty 17 year old daughter, Tina, a high school junior. Everyone's first impression of Tina was that from birth she was the girl who always got what she wanted...when she wanted it.

Tina's classmates joked that she was "the girl most likely to have been created by Satan." Her principal was heard to say, "If there was a picture in 'The Book Of Terminology And Sayings' to represent *Evil Incarnate*, it would be of Tina Evans."

Randomly picking blouses off a rack, Tina tossed them onto Ginger's already-loaded left arm while the mother obediently trotted behind her daughter.

As frustrating as it was, there was no way Ginger would attempt to discipline her only child. Since divorcing her first husband shortly after Tina's birth and retaining her maiden name for the two of them, Ginger never worked at being a parent. From the child's conception, Ginger wanted to be Tina's best friend.

But there were others in the Evans family who taught and trained the teenager on a *dark side*, a vicious and spiteful side...and Tina not only mastered it, she knew how to use it against her mother.

With blouses on hangers now covering both arms, Ginger tried to speak to her already pissed off daughter.

"I know you don't like him...but he's good. He's good to *me*...and he's been good to *you*."

Tina turned her back on her mother, not caring or listening, and walked to a rack of jeans.

Still trying to converse, but not loud enough for others to hear, Ginger near-pleaded, "Why can't you try?" In her mind she wanted to continue with, "You spoiled little bitch," but knew that would mean weeks of penance...so she kept her mouth shut.

Tina randomly picked up four pairs of jeans, turned to her mother, forcefully threw them to the floor and blared for all to hear, "I don't *want* to! I *told you!* I don't like him and I don't want him in my house!"

With several sets of eyes now on the Evans women, Ginger dumped the blouses onto the nearest rack, then rushed to her daughter and got on her knees to pick up the jeans. Tina looked down, sneering at her mother as she appeared to be groveling before her to those watching.

Ginger replaced the pants to the rack, then came close to her disrespectful daughter and began stroking her hair as if straightening it... at least that was what she wanted the still-watching customers to think.

In slightly-more-than-a-whisper, Ginger meagerly attempted to stand her ground.

"It's not *your* house. Steve and I bought it for *us*. For *our* future. Me and Steve. You're eventually going away to college. So for Christ-sake, Tina... can't you *try?*"

As loud as her last tirade, Tina bellowed, "*No!*"

Customers and store employees stopped what they were doing to eye the mother and daughter.

Still bearing her pissed off look, Tina headed for the front door with her mother following at a distance...much to everyone's happiness.

On the way to her Mercedes, Ginger continued the questioning.

"Why? Why do you hate him so much?"

Tina stopped, turned with eyes that looked like they could emit flames of anger, and said with a satanic growl in her teenage voice, "You *know* why."

The mother stood motionless in the parking lot, holding back tears as cars cautiously drove by her. She knew the conversation could go no further...though her daughter's wrath certainly would.

By the time a sullen Ginger made her way to the car, Tina was annoyed at having to wait for the doors to be unlocked. Once Ginger hit the remote, the 18 year old sat in the back, letting her mother know she didn't want to talk, and knowing it would crush Ginger to chauffeur her daughter, her best friend, home in silence.

"Drop me off at Nan's," came the command from the backseat of the Mercedes.

Those were the only words said by Tina as she endlessly texted during the 25 minute drive from the mall to Apple Hill, the upscale townhouse community in Ramsey, New Jersey where Ginger's sister and niece lived… only three short blocks from the unit Steve and Ginger bought less than a year earlier.

Nan was Laura 'Nan' Evans…the 71 year old mother of Ginger and Francine.

Francine was Ginger's older sister by six years. She was tall, and facially it was easy to see they were sisters…but Francine was always 60 pounds heavier, and she demanded everyone call her "Frank." Steve and Ginger privately joked that Francine resented not being born with testicles, but by using a male name it was the closest she'd get to owning a pair.

Once Steve and Ginger found their new residence, Nan ordered Francine to, "Find another one, a *bigger* one, as close to Tina as possible. You and Tabitha live there. I'll pay for it." And she did.

It was Laura who *really* raised her granddaughter after Ginger divorced Tina's father. The newly-single mother was an executive for a luggage manufacturer where her co-workers soon caught on that Ginger's rapid raise in salary and "relocation" to a large corner office was due to her long afternoon lunches at the local Ramada with the company's president.

And it was Laura who instilled a hatred for men in her daughters and granddaughters. But no one enjoyed learning to hate them more than Francine and Tina. To refer to Tina as the epitome of Evil Incarnate was only because the principal never met the teenager's grandmother or aunt. Had he known *them*, he would have re-evaluated his words and understood why Tina turned out the way she did.

Laura was a conniver. She always was. Especially when she married a man 23 years her senior whom she never loved. All that mattered was that he owned a lucrative cash business and wanted to have children. Laura just needed to make sure those children were girls. In the end, she got what she wanted. Twelve years earlier, her husband died unhappy at 82, regretting what his wife and daughters had become…and what he knew would become of his two granddaughters.

Inheriting the business, the bank accounts, a substantial stock and annuity portfolio, large paid-for homes in New Jersey and Florida, and a steamer trunk filled with unreported cash…Nan couldn't cremate him fast enough to begin enjoying the life she wanted for her and her brood.

The matriarch believed herself to be a domineering and powerful figure to all she met. Tall, a bad blonde dye-job with disturbing gray roots, gaudy rhinestone and zirconia jewelry, yet always well dressed, Laura sat in the kitchen of the townhouse she owned, but where Francine and her daughter Tabitha lived.

Ginger's car pulled away as Tina slammed her aunt's front door behind her, then bolted into the foyer and yelled, "She wants me to do what he says, Nan!"

Stomping into the kitchen, Tina sat at the dinette table. Her grandmother sympathetically pouted and reassuringly told her, "You don't have to do *anything* you don't want, honey. *Especially* for some man who's not your father."

"But she's telling me *I have to!*"

An almost maniacal glaze came over Laura's face. She lifted her head, raised her eyebrows, looked down her nose…and gave *"the stare."* The raising of their eyebrows was a family trait that appeared whenever the "Evans Girls" were up to no good.

In an almost feral growl, Laura looked at the teenager and murmured, "Leave your mother to me. *Nan* will take care of it." Then she tightly hugged Tina and whispered so no one else in the house could hear, "You *know* you're my favorite."

That was all Tina needed to hear. Once they separated with a kiss on each other's cheek, the plotting child happily rose and walked out the door she slammed only a few moments earlier.

Francine entered the kitchen from the hallway where she stood eavesdropping on their conversation…though not hearing her mother whisper to Tina. As if permanently attached to Francine's hip was Tabitha, her 16 year old, tall, thin, dark-haired and perpetually bored.

Seventeen years earlier Francine quickly became pregnant during her very-brief marriage...though Ginger and Steve often joked that it was the *only* time and the *last* time the older Evans sister "got laid."

Moments after returning from the obstetrician's office with the results of her amniocentesis, Francine and her mother called the family's lawyer. Knowing her child would be female, Francine then called her husband and said, "Your clothes are outside the door. I got what I wanted and I'm filing for divorce. I *never* want to see you again."

Within a few months of Tabitha's birth, Francine was single...and the child was given her mother's last name. The father never saw his daughter. He rapidly became an alcoholic, lost his job, his home, and at 42 years old had no option but to move in with his aging, sick parents.

As she sat across from Laura and with Tabitha standing next to them, Francine expressed with equal amounts of concern and evil, "I'm telling you, Mom, Ginger knows Tina's wrong. So how are you going to get her to tell Steve *he's* wrong?"

With conviction in her voice, the matriarch answered, "There's got to be something we can do. I promised Tina." Then she raised her eyebrows and gave *the stare*. "I'll do *anything* for my granddaughters...just like I did for you and your sister." Her look of anger and determination grew stronger as she went on, "Who's *he* to want respect from my Tina? What's *he* know about being a parent?" The same evil that emitted from Tina's eyes appeared in Laura's. "Whatever it takes to teach Steve a lesson, Francine... I'll do it."

Three days later in the dining room of the Steve Meyers and Ginger Evans townhouse, Ginger prepared three place settings for dinner when the sound of the front door opening and closing lit up her face.

"Ginge!" was heard from the foyer.

"In here, Steve!" she called back.

Steve Meyers was 45 years old, handsome with a twinkle of 'constant youth' in his eyes, and always dressed well due to his corporate job, and because he always wanted to look good for his wife. It never bothered him that she didn't take his last name after they married. He knew Ginger loved him and only kept the Evans name because of her child.

At least that was what *he* believed.

Putting down his suitcase and briefcase, Steve made his way into the dining room where they rushed to each other, romantically kissing and embracing.

"How was your day?" Steve asked once their lips separated.

"Better now that *you're* back."

Just as they started another round of kissing Steve smelled smoke. Cigarette smoke.

Seeing Tina at the other end of the room holding a Marlboro and staring at Ginger with her grandmother's burning eyes, Steve held back any sign of anger or frustration as she blew a bigger cloud in their direction.

"C'mon, Tina," Steve said as calmly as he could, knowing it was falling on deaf ears. "We've asked you not to smoke in the house, haven't we? Would you *please* put it out…or take it outside?"

Tina didn't move. She stood…staring at her mother who was visibly unable to look at or speak to her daughter. Steve couldn't tell if his wife was ashamed to look at the child…or afraid.

To break the tension, he scanned the table settings, did his best to smile and returned his eyes to his step-daughter. Trying to hold back the strain in his voice, he asked, "You're eating with us?"

Tina dropped the cigarette on the hardwood floor, ground it out with a vengeance, then walked up the steps to her bedroom.

Ginger burst into tears. Without saying a word, she ran to the kitchen to get what was needed to clean the floor, leaving Steve to stand there holding back his anger for both of them. He wanted to tell the spoiled, undisciplined child she was ruining his marriage, his home, his job…and his life.

But he also knew his pain would only result in Tina's happiness. And that hurt him even more.

Later that evening Steve and Ginger made their way upstairs to the master bedroom. He walked past several of his favorite possessions…pieces of art, his memorabilia collection and exquisitely framed family photos that went back four generations, all adorning the walls of every room in the townhouse.

As they undressed, Steve told his wife, "I have to go to Cleveland again, Ginge. But this'll be *the one*. It's taken a lot of work, but if everything clicks and they sign the contract, it should bring in a nice bonus. And when it does..." He proudly and lovingly smiled at the woman he adored, and continued, "...we're going to Maui for the honeymoon I promised you a couple of years ago."

Ginger, now naked, walked to her husband and held him close. She was *very* proud of him.

Though she had a pretty face with hair and attire that always made her attractive, once Ginger was out of her clothes there was nothing anyone would call 'sexy' about her. It bothered her that she wasn't blessed with anything to speak of that would be considered breasts. Conversely, her ass was spreading to a noticeable extreme, and unknown to everyone was the twinge of jealousy Ginger felt over the last few years about her daughter's already-adult and filled-out physique. Ginger's logic, whenever she felt the need to comment on her less-than-small breasts and larger-than-normal ass was, "At least I'm not as fat as my sister."

But Steve was in love with her simply for her...not for any physical features.

While in his embrace, Ginger's look changed to concern as she asked, "What about Tina?" which caused Steve's expression to be replaced by one of sadness.

"You know she won't want to go, even if it *is* to Hawaii. Not as long as *I'm* there. And if we take her, it's just gonna ruin the time we need together. Can't she stay here...with your mother and sister?"

His wife squeezed him tighter and sighed...knowing what he just asked for would be the beginning of his death sentence.

Sitting in the comfortable window-seat of her bedroom, blowing cigarette smoke outside and weeping into her cell-phone was Tina.

"I don't want him here, Frank! I don't want to live here as long as he's here. You're three blocks away...can't I move in with you and Tabitha?"

Aunt Francine was sitting at her kitchen table on the house-line's speakerphone, and though it was nearly 11PM, she was eating Vanilla Fudge ice cream from the container. Laura sat across from her, and 16 year old Tabitha was in the living room watching Ren & Stimpy reruns while eating from a bucket of freshly-made popcorn, regardless of it being a school night.

In a hopeful, yet somewhat demented way, Francine queried, "Why? *Did he touch you?*" Her niece's response of "No" brought disappointment to Francine's face.

Tina continued with, "I just want my mother back…and I don't want *him* in the house."

Knowing it would push just *one* of Tina's buttons, Francine said, "Your mother's happy with him. She's happy with the house, and--"

"*I don't care!*" came the furious response Francine hoped for, renewing the smile to her face.

Wanting to reassure the teenager, Francine said, "Don't worry, honey. Me and Nan will come up with something, but--"

"But *what?*" Tina interrupted, now with audible tears coming through the speaker.

"This is the second husband you're making us get rid of, Tina. You gotta realize your mom's not going back with your father. You've got to--"

Still at the window, Tina yelled, "*I want him out of here! You know why! Just do it!*" not caring who heard it…then disconnected the call, angrily slammed down the phone and took a long, hard drag on her cigarette.

In the kitchen three blocks away, Francine turned off the speakerphone, raised her eyebrows as high as they could go, then looked across the table to watch her mother's brows do the same, only higher…and more sinister.

Standing on the front porch, Steve Meyers wore his corporate attire and noticed the spectacular mid-May sunrise. The limo driver took Steve's suitcase and briefcase from the foyer to the stretch that would take him to Newark International Airport for his 7:15AM flight to Cleveland.

Ginger, in a robe and holding a cup of coffee, sidled up behind her husband, rested her face on his back and rubbed it around. He was happy to feel her there.

"Wish me luck, Ginge. If this goes like it should, we're off to paradise."

She walked around to face him, looked into his eyes, then deeply hugged and kissed him before saying, "I love you, Steve. Just remember that…okay?"

His heart filled as he amorously nodded and walked to the waiting limo's open rear door.

Sitting in the upstairs window-seat was Tina, again with the phone to an ear, a cigarette hanging from her mouth, and her eyes staring at the long vehicle in the street.

Once the limo started to pull away, Steve lowered the rear window and waved to his wife. Ginger waved back, however…there was a sadness in her eyes he couldn't see.

"He's gone," the teenager blurted into the phone.

A day later, while Steve was in Cleveland, Ginger, Francine and Laura sat at a wooden table on the rear deck of Steve and Ginger's townhouse, picking and eating pieces of fruit from a bowl as they spoke. With them were their apprentices, Tina and Tabitha.

Of course, Tabitha sat as close to her mother as physically possible without actually being on her lap, and Tina showed her allegiance by sitting between her Aunt Francine and grandmother. It made Ginger unhappy not to have her daughter next to her.

In an attempt to save her third marriage, Ginger called the meeting to speak her mind. Eyeing her mother and sister as she spoke, she did the best she could.

"Maybe it's time Tina *didn't* get her way," eventually came from her mouth.

The Evans stare erupted in unison from Francine and Laura…with Laura taking immediate control.

Putting an arm around her granddaughter, Laura snarled, "*No!* There's no reason why this child has to kiss your husband's ass."

Ginger tried to defend her statement with, "She's not a child, Mom! She'll be eighteen on her next birthday. And Steve doesn't want his ass kissed. But he *does* deserve a 'thank you' or a 'please' when she talks to him. Doesn't he deserve *some* respect? Something for giving her a nice place to live? Food? Clothes? He pays for her cell-phone, for Christ-sake! The same phone she uses to call and text you two to tell you how much she hates him."

With a wicked glare, Francine said to her mother, "I *told you* this wasn't gonna be easy. Look! She loves him."

"Of *course* I love him," the younger sister snapped back. "He's good to me. He's good to *Tina*. He hasn't done *anything*. And what he *did* do…we, the three of us, *told him to do!* Why do *I* have to get divorced again? Why can't *I* be happy?"

As soon as Ginger finished, Laura had her reply ready.

"Because just like I taught each of you, I'm going to teach your daughters that *no* man is worth being unhappy over. Don't you *ever* forget that! You're *all* my girls and we'll *always* be together. I carved that lesson into your father, and I'll do it to *anyone* who comes between us! When you first brought Steve home, I told him…" Out came the evil, burning eyes. "'If you *ever* make *any* of my girls unhappy…I'll ruin you.'" Slowing her words to emphasize her anger, she closed in on Ginger and declared, "And my Tina is unhappy."

Tina moved her chair closer to her grandmother…pissing Ginger off even more.

Ginger didn't give up, this time raising her voice a little more…knowing the inevitable consequences.

"She's *my* Tina, Mom! And *no!* She's not unhappy…she's *spoiled!* You just don't want to see it. You don't want to admit it. You don't want to admit you and Frank *made her* that way!"

As if it were an involuntary reaction, Laura's hand appeared from nowhere and slapped Ginger's face.

Hard.

With Francine and Tabitha shocked at what they just witnessed, Tina quickly turned away…to smile.

Before Ginger could react, Laura raised her eyebrows and commanded, "My granddaughter's unhappy, so we're getting rid of him…and that's it!"

While Ginger held her reddened, hand-marked face, Francine put her arm around Tabitha. The three looked down…knowing the meeting was over and nothing more would be said about it.

Laura and Tina looked at one another.
They had won.

CHAPTER 4

Some *More* Backstory – The Decline & Fall Of Steve Meyers

It was early Saturday afternoon on May 21ˢᵗ, 2016, when Ginger found her husband sitting at the kitchen table. He had gone to the mailbox as he did every Saturday to collect what was usually junk mail, bills and catalogs. Returning from Cleveland two days earlier, Steve was looking forward to relaxing over the weekend, but the envelope in his hand was about to change his life.

It was about to change his life…forever.

"Are you okay, Steve?" she asked the shocked, motionless man.

Ginger stood in the archway between the foyer and kitchen, unsure if she needed to call an ambulance.

Steve softly articulated, "I looked at it, then put it back in. I waited for you."

Not sure of what it could be, but worried it came from her mother or Tina, she approached Steve, placed a hand on his shoulder and said, "Show me."

Spreading open the envelope, he took out a piece of paper and a check, then, as if not believing it, said, "It came today. I didn't expect it so soon. We only signed the contract on Tuesday. It's more than I thought. *Double* more than I thought. Twenty-four thousand dollars, Ginge! *After* taxes. And look…a note from the CEO."

He unfolded the paper and read, "'To our man Steve Meyers. For going above and beyond in Cleveland. It couldn't have happened without you. We're grateful to have you on our team.'"

Delighted of her husband's achievement, Ginger hugged and kissed him.

"You deserve it, Steve. You worked *very* hard for it and I'm *very* proud of you." Then, in a rare sexual twist, she said, "Tina went with Frank and Tabitha to a couple of malls. How about we go back to bed?"

He instinctively grinned and stood up. Holding each other's hand, like teenagers they hurried upstairs.

The next day, Steve happily drove himself across the New Jersey border into West Nyack, New York to do a little clothes shopping for Maui at the Palisades Center Mall. Due to Bergen County's Blue Laws it was easier to make the 20 minute drive into another state than to deal with traffic on Routes 17 and 46 to shop in the non-Blue Law Jersey counties.

Unfortunately, that left his wife in the grips of *the dark side*.

The congress of schemers, Francine, Laura and Tina had Ginger once again sitting across from them on her back deck. Tabitha was there, but was bored and it was evident she didn't possess the same dominant *evil-gene* as her mother, grandmother and cousin. But she still positioned herself as close to her mother as the laws of physics would allow.

"Twenty-four thousand? *Now?*" growled Laura, staring at her younger daughter. "That's bad, Ginger. You've got to get to Hawaii right away, and I mean *right away*. Pay the most you can for airline tickets. You've got to spend every god-damn-penny of that check. He can't have *any* of it for a lawyer by the time you get back. I want you to find the most expensive hotel. Eat at expensive restaurants…and spend as much as you can."

It didn't take long for Laura's *stare* to return once she leaned close to Ginger and snarled, "I want him broke. Do you hear me? *Broke.*"

There was no responding. Ginger just closed her eyes and bowed her head. Inside, she was bursting into tears…but she couldn't let these women see it.

Once Ginger's head was down, Laura winked at Tina, who smiled back knowing her grandmother had everything under control.

Needing to break the silence, and wanting information she and her mother could use to start their plotting, Francine asked, "What does Steve cherish most?"

The question caused Ginger's tears to flow. Raising her head, the sobbing wife replied, "*Me.*" Wiping her eyes, she resumed with, "Making me happy. Our home. His job. Why, Frank?"

Before anyone could respond, Tina sadistically tossed in, "Don't forget those shitty pictures and art-stuff. The house is *loaded* with them," which caused her mother to cry a little harder.

Francine didn't respond, though she *did* raise her eyebrows and gaze at her already-scheming mother.

It was very early on Saturday, May 28th, only seven days after receiving his bonus check, when Steve stepped out of the master bedroom making sure he had everything that needed to be in his possession for a fifteen day vacation. Cash, credit cards, cell-phone, boarding passes and keys for the locked luggage. As he strolled along the hallway and down the stairs to the foyer, he admired the art and photos on the walls.

The limo driver loaded their check-on and carry-on bags into the trunk of the stretch as Steve came down to find the Evans gang. He and Ginger were dressed for their early morning ten-and-a-half hour flight from Newark to the Honolulu International Airport, followed by a short layover before the one hour hop to Maui's Kahului Airport. Once there, they would pick up their rented Jaguar convertible and drive another forty minutes to the hotel. It was going to be a very long day.

Based on their performances, it would be hard for anyone to believe Steve was not loved by *all* of the women before him.

Laura, Francine and Tabitha surrounded the happy couple, giving wishes for a great trip, suggestions to take a lot of pictures, and to not worry about *anything* because they'll take care of Tina and the townhouse.

Tina wasn't in the foyer. Though able to see and be seen by everyone, she stood in the kitchen smoking a cigarette and making it obvious she didn't want to be near them. Of course, it had nothing to do with her concern of causing secondhand smoke.

Kissing and hugging Ginger, Laura excitedly said, "You kids have a wonderful time! Just be careful and enjoy yourselves." When she hugged Steve, she was facing Ginger and said, "Don't worry about a thing, Steve. Me and Frank will take care of *everything*," as she gave her daughter a knowing wink behind his back.

With Laura, Francine and Tabitha standing in the doorway watching the couple make their way down the steps to the limo, Francine sinisterly quipped, "Yep… *everything*."

Steve stepped aside to let Ginger enter the limo first. As he was about to slide in, Tina stood next to her grandmother and asked, "Will he be gone soon, Nan?"

"Look at him now, sweetheart. It's the last time you'll *ever* see him smiling," replied the matriarch-from-hell with a vile self-gratifying grin on her aged face.

On a United 747 heading west at 37,000 feet, and several hours into the flight, Steve and Ginger, hand-in-hand since taking off, were enjoying champagne in their First Class seats.

Already having two more flutes than he should have, Steve passionately kissed his wife, then sat back into the comfortable leather seat. Rarely consuming alcohol at home, work or socially, Steve Meyers was not known for being a drinker.

Speaking from his heart, but with the assistance of the alcohol, he kept his voice low enough for only Ginger to hear and said, "I hope when we get back...we can make this family work."

Not being a conversation she wanted to have, Ginger did her best to act coy and responded affectionately with, "Let it go, honey. Let's just enjoy ourselves, okay?"

That wasn't the answer he, or the alcohol, wanted to hear, so his reply was a little irate.

"C'mon, it's been two years, Ginge! *Two years!* And it was your mother and sister's idea. I did it for *them!* For *you!* You *asked* me to do it. Why does Tina hold it against *me?*"

Lashing out for bringing up a sore subject, she retorted, "Because you're the one who told Kyle to go away...not *them.*"

Raising his head to make sure no one was listening, he looked at her and let a little more ire come through.

"She was fifteen, for Christ-sake. We caught them..." He looked around again, lowered his angry voice and finished. "...fucking in her room."

His wife barked so the surrounding rows could hear, "Quiet! You're drunk!"

It was too late. Steve took a mouthful of champagne, swallowed and decided *this* was the time for this conversation.

"Shit, Ginge! Even *I* fucked some fifteen year old in her parents' house. But *I was fifteen too*. Kyle was *twenty-two*." He finished what little remained in his flute and continued, "At least we were smart enough to do it when her parents weren't comin' home."

Ginger made it clear to *everyone* within viewing and hearing distance she no longer wanted to be part of the conversation, nor hear anything disparaging about her daughter. She yelled, "Be quiet! It's history. Leave it alone," then turned away, acting as if she wanted to go to sleep.

The volume and her words caught the attention of the two flight attendants.

But Steve wasn't done.

With his voice audible to others, he slurred, "Ever since that day, your kid's been wishing I'd keel over and die. I didn't care that Kyle was black. You *know* that didn't matter to me. But he *lied* to us, Ginge. He told us... he told *you* he was seventeen. He was twenty-fucking-two and fuckin' a fifteen year old."

Ginger, getting angrier by the second, refused to turn and face him, which only gave him the opportunity to finish what he wanted to say.

"It freaked *your mother* out that he was black. *That's* why she wanted him gone. It embarrassed *her*. Not *us*."

Still facing away, she shrieked, "Stop it, Steve!" causing the First Class passengers and flight attendants to again look in their direction.

He reached, took Ginger's half-filled flute, downed it and kept going, "Face it... Tina needs some kind of counseling. She needs a fuckin' shrink. Your daughter's ruining our marriage."

That was it. Ginger spun around. The *stare* was already there. Her eyebrows were raised to the middle of her forehead, and for the first time, the flames her mother, sister and daughter were so good at had finally shown in Ginger's eyes as she glared at her husband.

Normally, men would run from such a sight. But Steve's frustration had been building for years, and between the alcohol and the fact Ginger was his captive-audience during the flight, he looked around, again lowered his voice and remained on the topic as her eyes burned into him.

"After you three had me threaten him with some statutory-rape-*bullshit*, he never came around again. Your mother thought I was King-Fucking-

Shit. She treated me like I was some kind of fucking savior. At least that's what she *wanted* me to believe. It was like I saved her granddaughter from some fate worse than fuckin' death…because *none of you* had the balls to tell your precious-fucking-Tina to break up with the poor bastard. The three of you had *me* do it."

With eyebrows still raised, she heatedly asked, "Are you done now?"

He was. But the alcohol *wasn't*.

Staring at Ginger with *his own* angry eyes, Steve snarled, "Once Kyle was gone…Tina wanted me dead," then turned his back on the evil *Evans stare* and closed his eyes.

To the appreciation of everyone in the First Class cabin, the champagne took its toll and Steve slept for the rest of the flight.

Though it was a little after 9PM in New Jersey, it was six hours earlier in Maui. The ebony black Jaguar F-Type convertible pulled into the driveway of the Grand Wialea Hotel on Maui and was rapidly surrounded by valets, bellmen and a bell captain.

The car was swiftly emptied of luggage and driven away as Steve and Ginger were draped in leis and escorted to the front desk within the open-air lobby that resembled an art and sculpture gallery bordered by a tropical rainforest.

A few moments later, the couple was led to the elevator by a bellman with their luggage cart. He was to take them to their ocean view suite on the 8th floor.

While standing in the rising elevator, a very tired, hungry, jet-lagged and hungover Steve Meyers read the receipt he had just signed and gave his credit card to in order to cover the total upon checking out.

"Really, Ginge? Do we *really* need a suite for seven-eighty-five a night? For two weeks? And a Jaguar?"

Not wanting to have this conversation, she quickly countered with, "It's supposed to be our honeymoon, Steve…and it was a package. That's why we had to come so soon. Please, stop bitching about it. Can't we just have a good time?"

"But eleven grand, Ginge? For a friggin' room? Our whole *wedding* didn't come to that."

Sensing the extreme tension in the confined space, the bellman offered, "It *is* an ocean view suite, sir. Probably one of the best on the island."

Steve scanned the tall employee, then said, "Do they pay you to say shit like that? 'Cause if you open your mouth one more time, you can either get your fuckin' tip from *them*, or you can walk outta our hot-shit ocean view suite holding your jaw and missing a couple of teeth."

Ginger's head rose in astonishment and she looked at her husband. In all the years they were together, she never heard him speak to *anyone* like that. She didn't know if she should have been turned on by it...or afraid.

The elevator doors parted and Ginger was the first one out, saying, "Let's go. We have scuba lessons in an hour, and dinner reservations at eight."

Before they stepped out, Steve leaned toward the bellman and asked, "Any chance scuba lessons are included in the room rate?"

The response was negative...then they followed Ginger down the hall to the ocean view suite.

It *was* one of the best on the island.

Thirteen days later, while making arrangements at the marina for a sailboat ride, a tanned and relaxed Steve went to pay as an equally-tanned Ginger, with the saddest of faces, stood in the parking lot talking on her cell-phone. It was important her husband not hear what was being discussed.

"The limo will pick us up in Newark and we should be home by eleven on Sunday night, then..." Holding back tears, she tried to continue without giving her pain away, "...Steve leaves for Cleveland the next morning. He'll be home four days later."

With ecstatic happiness in her voice, her sister said, "We'll start cleaning the place out as soon as he leaves. Stay strong. Mom's handling *everything*. Tina's happier than she's been in years." Sensing Ginger's concern, she finished with, "You *know* what you're doing is right."

Summoning what little energy she could muster to argue with Francine, Ginger countered, "No it's *not*, Frank! It's not what's right for me...*or* Steve."

"It is for Tina!" Francine barked back.

Though peeved at her sister's response, Ginger saw her husband walk out of the marina's office, so she yelled into the phone, but as softly as possible, "It's not for her either! It's for *Mom*...and you know it!" She disconnected the call, slid the phone into her purse and nervously slipped on sunglasses to cover her tear-filled eyes.

Steve approached behind her...and he couldn't look or be happier.

"I got the tickets. The boat leaves in twenty minutes. Is everything okay?"

His wife regained her composure as best she could, then turned, gave him a half-hearted smile and answered, "Yeah. Everyone said 'Hello,' and they can't wait to hear about the trip."

"Didja tell them we're having a great time?"

All she could do was nod.

He couldn't hold back his exhilaration. Hugging his wife, Steve whispered in her ear, "I love you, Ginge. I truly love you."

She hoped he couldn't tell she was crying as they embraced.

Carrying luggage, the limo driver followed Steve and Ginger into the foyer. Turning on the lights in the kitchen, Steve called out, "Tina! We're home!"

The driver returned to the car for the rest of the bags as Ginger said, though feeling guilty while saying it, "She's staying at my sister's tonight."

Disappointed, Steve said, "I guess I'll see her when I get back. I have her presents."

Feeling *more* guilty, she assured him, "Don't worry. I'll...I'll give them to her for you."

Once the driver returned with the remaining luggage, Steve paid him and confirmed that he would be picked up the following morning for his trip to Cleveland.

Ginger quickly and quietly went upstairs into the master bathroom, locked the door and turned on the shower to cover the sound as she sat on the toilet and cried.

It was Friday, June 10th...the rainy evening Steve returned from Cleveland that would change his life.

It was the night that would crush him.

Still in his suit, he carried his luggage from the car and up the steps to the front of his townhouse. All the lights were out, which he thought was odd.

Unlocking the door, he stepped in from the rain, placed his briefcase on the floor and turned on the foyer and stairway lights. Carrying the suitcase, he walked up the steps and called out, "Ginge! I'm home!"

There was no reply.

Entering the master bedroom, he turned on the light, threw the suitcase on the bed and eyed the clock. It was 10:53PM…and he was worried. He went to the night table, grabbed the phone and dialed…but an answering machine picked up on the first ring.

"Hello. Francine and Tabitha aren't home. Leave a message and we'll call you back."

BEEP.

Not hiding the nervousness in his voice out of concern for his wife, he said, "Hi Frank, it's Steve. Guess you girls are out somewhere."

Three blocks away and surrounding the answering machine on the kitchen table were the triumvirate of connivers, Laura, Francine and Tina, with eyebrows raised and wicked grins staring at the speaker as if it were meat…and they were a pride of starving lions. Tabitha couldn't care less as she watched Ren & Stimpy reruns in the living room and ate popcorn.

Ginger stood to the side…sad. Sad as she had never been sad before.

Steve continued, "Do me a favor…tell Ginger I'm home and I can't wait to see her. Thanks."

Then he hung up.

All eyes and eyebrows turned to Ginger.

Laura spoke the words, "Make the call," causing tears to stream down Ginger's face.

From the time Steve hung up the phone, it was less than fifteen minutes before the doorbell rang. Still in the bedroom unpacking, he smiled when he heard it. Assuming his wife went shopping and her hands were too full to open the door, still in his suit, he rushed down the stairs and swung the door open.

His face changed to 'worry' when he saw a Police Sergeant and two patrolmen standing in the rain. Looking past them, he saw two police cars in the street...with their lights flashing.

The Sergeant stepped forward and asked, "Are you Steven Meyers?"

"Oh no! What happened to Ginger?" Steve cried out.

"Are you Steven Meyers?" the Sergeant reiterated.

"Yes! What happened to my wife?"

Hearing what they needed to hear, the patrolmen stepped into the foyer, took Steve's arms, pushed him face-first against the wall causing blood to trickle from his nose, spread his arms and legs apart and frisked him.

"What the fuck are you doing?" the confused husband yelled.

Once frisked, they pulled his arms behind him and handcuffed the now-freaking out Steve.

"Do you own a firearm, Mr. Meyers?" the Sergeant asked.

Fighting against the handcuffs, he was getting frantic as he asked, "What's going on? Where's *my wife?*"

"I said, 'Do you own a weapon?'"

"And *I* said, '*What's going on?*' and '*Where's my wife?*'"

One of the patrolmen slammed Steve into the wall and commanded, "Answer the Sergeant."

With blood running from his nose, Steve muttered, "Upstairs. In the office. In the closet. It's in a case. Locked...like it's supposed to be. The key's in the desk. Top drawer. Why?"

The Sergeant nodded to the other patrolman who ran upstairs. Then the two policemen led Steve into the kitchen. Once the patrolman flipped the light switch, each man was surprised by what they saw.

The table was on its side. Its six chairs were strewn about the room. Potted plants and dirt were all over the floor. Pictures on the wall were askew. It appeared something violent happened while Steve was gone.

Confused, scared and with blood trickling from his nose, Steve turned to the patrolman and asked, "What happened? Where's my wife?" Not getting a response, he turned to the Sergeant and begged, "What happened to her? Where's Ginger?"

The Sergeant walked to the kitchen sink, grabbed a few paper towels, rolled over one of the chairs and sat Steve into it. The lawman wiped blood off Steve's face, then took out a folded document and held it in front of the prisoner.

Steve looked at it, but had no idea what was going on.

"It's a Restraining Order," the Sergeant said with no emotion.

"For *what?*"

The patrolman returned from upstairs carrying a pistol case, and reported, "It's in here. Everything, like he said."

The Sergeant got in front of Steve and explained why they were there.

"Mr. Meyers, yesterday your wife and her attorney appeared before a County judge and charged that you assaulted her a few days ago, and you threatened her with the weapon in that bag."

Stupefied and at a near-loss for words, Steve mustered, "But…but I was in Cleveland. Look at me! I'm still wearing *my suit*. My suitcase is still on the bed. How the fuck could I assault her?"

"According to this document, evidence was provided, a decision was made by a judge, and you've been ordered to immediately vacate the premises."

Trying to grasp the reality of what was happening, and also trying to be rational in front of the policemen, Steve sought to calmly explain his case.

"I can't leave here, Sergeant. My office is here. It's upstairs. I *work* out of here. All my files, my computer, everything I need for my job is up there. This is *insane*."

The cops had a job to do, and no matter what Steve might have said, it was their job to remove him from his home.

"Take whatever you need as long as you get it together in five minutes. You and your lawyer need to be in court in a couple of weeks. It's all on that paper. Then you can tell your side to the judge…not to me."

Steve was numb. He had no idea what just happened…or why.

Speaking to him man-to-man, the Sergeant stared Steve in the eyes and said, "Look, Mr. Meyers…I don't care if you're innocent or not. All I can tell you is this…we do this two or three times a month. Sometimes *more*. It's pretty common. A marriage has a problem and one spouse files an R.O. to piss off the other." Then he looked at the mess the kitchen was in and continued, "Something must've gotten up your wife's ass…and she's nailing *you* for it."

Still confused, bleeding and with his hands secured behind his back, Steve nodded toward the overturned table and said, holding back tears, "It wasn't like this when I left."

"Look…you're wasting time. Get some clothes together, 'cause I gotta get you outta here. I don't know if it's bullshit or not, but I got orders that your wife has a kid that needs to get to bed." Then the Sergeant turned to one of the patrolmen and said, "Take the cuffs off."

That was when the reality of everything that was happening struck Steve like a lightning bolt.

Neighbors stood in the rain watching the police officers walk Steve and a suitcase out of his townhouse. The Sergeant was holding the pistol case.

Water pelted the frightened and confused Steve as he got in his car. The Sergeant stood between him and the open door and said, "If you beat the Restraining Order, you'll get the gun back. But I'm telling you for your own good…stay away from her. If she reports that you call or bother her, you're gonna get arrested and go to jail. Got that?"

There was nothing Steve could do but nod his head…and cry.

With their lights flashing, the police followed his car out of Apple Hill, and stayed behind him until it was across the Bergen County line.

Except for Ginger, it was a happy day for the Evans girls.

CHAPTER 5

When Evil Meets Corruptible

It was Thursday, June 23rd, 2016, when Laura Evans walked into the not very well kept and stuffy office of a Hoboken, New Jersey attorney with a not-very-successful career. Walking past the nearly-braindead receptionist, Laura entered the inner office of the man she came to see.

A cheaply framed law degree was surrounded by pictures of children on the stained wall behind a shabbily dressed, tall, obese man sitting at his desk.

Laura made sure to close the door behind her. What she had to say was for his ears only. She sat across from the Zoloft-popping Irving Pollack, a stressed out lawyer in his early 40s who looked to be closer to 60. His suit hadn't seen a dry-cleaner since it was purchased and his hands shook from a cocktail of prescribed pharmaceutical medications.

After she introduced herself, the attorney leaned back in his worn leather chair and said, "Mrs. Evans, I don't know why you're here. We shouldn't even be talking. Steve's my friend and my client…there are ethics involved."

Within a millisecond she shot back with, "Cut the shit, Pollack," and rapidly took control of the conversation. "You're a lawyer. Don't try to bullshit me about *ethics*. Besides, that's not important right now. What you should be more concerned about is the fact that we *both* know your client has no money…and *I* know you'll never get paid."

"That's only because Ginger emptied their bank accounts and stock portfolios while he was in Cleveland. You know that," he replied.

Her eyebrows rose just a bit as she asked, "Do you think he'll *ever* be able to pay you?"

"Keeping him out of the house was the key to *that*. The poor mensch has been walking around with his head up his ass. He's *bound* to get fired if he doesn't get everything that's upstairs in his office." Then the lawyer shook his head in pity for his friend and continued, "Your daughter really knew what she was doing when she set him up like that. But I'm sure he'll get his due share from the court."

Feeling confident in himself, he sat back and watched Laura reach into a large Louis Vuitton purse and take out a stuffed manila envelope.

"What's the most you can bill him? Ten? Fifteen thousand? And then *hope* you'll get it?" she asked, placing the envelope on his desk.

"That's not open for discussion, Mrs. Evans. I'll get paid after the Property Settlement when their divorce goes to court in eighteen months. January, two-thousand-eighteen."

She gave her trademark sinister smile, shook her head and said, "There won't be any Property Settlement, Mr. Pollack."

"What makes you say that?" he asked with interest.

She slid the envelope toward him. His eyes went wide once he opened it and looked inside.

"Thirty-one thousand dollars...in cash. It's from the sale of some of that art and old crap he collected that he'll never see again."

"That's marital property! *None* of those pieces should have been sold." Then he held up the envelope and suspiciously asked, "And this is for?"

Again, her response was immediate.

"*You* figure it out." She looked around the sloppy office and said, almost laughing, "Use it to fix up this place. Take your kids to Disney World. I don't care." Then she stood, walked to the door, turned to face him and said with vengeance in her voice, "And just so you know...Ginger had *nothing* to do with keeping Steve out of the house so he could lose his job, his money *or* his mind." Raising her eyebrows to the extreme, she gave him *the stare*...and it scared him. She went on, "Should you *try* to win tomorrow's Restraining Order hearing *or* the divorce, you'll be going up against *me*, Mr. Pollack...not my daughter. And trust me...you'll lose."

The lawyer sat speechless as Laura grabbed the doorknob, then stopped and said, "Remember *this*. No matter what happens or what's said in court..." Her eyes burned through him. "...*nothing* is to be said about my granddaughter."

Finally opening the door, Laura Evans walked out...much to the lawyer's relief.

Pollack immediately opened his top drawer, took out a bottle of pills and swallowed two. Then he eyed the cash one more time and thought for a few seconds before slipping the envelope into a tattered briefcase next to the desk. Shaking his head in personal disappointment and disgust, he tapped the button on the intercom and said to the receptionist, "Bring in Steve Meyers' file."

Laura Evans had taken the final step to destroying another man's life.

The following morning started off hot and humid as Steve Meyers and Irving Pollack, the man Steve knew for years and considered his friend, the man he hired to protect and look out for his best interest, the man who swore to guide him through the evil, treacherous world of "law," walked up the marble steps of Hackensack's Bergen County Courthouse to defend Steve against the charges that he had assaulted and threatened Ginger.

The courtroom was like every other in similar buildings, and like them, sat dozens of '*the unconcerned*'...until it was their turn for justice.

Sitting in the third row on the center aisle was the Delivery Man.

Judge Louis Falzone, an aged man of 72...who looked every day of it, presided on the bench.

A *very* confused and distraught Steve sat at the defendant's table beside his anxiety filled, yet medicated attorney.

Ginger Evans, well dressed as always, but visibly stressed, was on the witness stand. The very slick, shapely, mid-40s prosecuting attorney, May Shapiro, had just finished questioning Ginger and returned to the plaintiff's table.

Behind Shapiro, in the first row of the gallery, sat *The Club*...Laura, Tina, Francine and Tabitha. Each was made-up and dressed to the nines.

Laura gave a sly smile and wink to the judge. He saw it. It registered. But he knew not to show a reaction or response.

"Counselor," Judge Falzone bellowed in Pollack's direction, "Begin your cross examination."

Whether it was due to the medication, or that he was nervous about being in front of the judge, or because he was afraid of Ginger's mother... Pollack's hands shook as he picked up a blank legal pad and apprehensively began his questioning.

"Miss Meyers, I'd like you to tell us--"

"It's Evans," Ginger interrupted.

"Pardon?" Pollack timidly asked.

"It's Evans. Ginger *Evans*," she said, irritated by his mistake.

The judge stepped in.

"Counselor, did you *read* the charges? Are you aware of the name the plaintiff filed them under?"

Irving stuttered over his words until he was able to get out, "Uh...yes, your honor. I'm sorry." He rustled through some papers on the table, then confessed, "I seem to have left a few documents back in my office."

That statement concerned Steve enough to say, a little too loud, "Back at your *office?*" as he put his head in his hands.

Laura and Francine grinned. Tina had been glaring at Steve from the minute he entered the courtroom. Tabitha...as usual, was bored.

Steve pulled at his attorney's sleeve, causing Pollack to lean down and listen to what his client whispered. Standing up, he eyed Ginger and asked, "Miss Evans, did you take your *first* husband's last name?"

"No."

There was a quiet pause...as if Pollack didn't know what to ask next. Again Steve pulled the sleeve and whispered to Pollack, who stubbornly shook his head in disagreement. Steve's expression changed to sheer anger... as if commanding his friend and defender without saying a word.

Pollack nervously glanced at Ginger and continued, "When your daughter Tina was born to that marriage, you didn't give *her* your husband's last name...her biological father, is that correct?"

Answering "Correct" with such perfection and precision as she did sounded as if Ginger had been trained to do so.

Looking into the gallery where *The Club* was sitting, fear abruptly appeared on Pollack's face upon seeing Laura's raised eyebrows and eyes that were burning into him for mentioning Tina. The Delivery Man noticed Pollack's reaction at seeing her, causing him to realize Laura was someone to keep *his* eyes on.

Steve grabbed Pollack's sleeve *again*. The attorney leaned in as Steve whispered, "Ask her how long she stayed married after the kid was born."

Frightened to do as Steve said, Pollack again shook his head and showed resistance.

"*Ask her!*" Steve said forcefully, causing those nearby to look at him.

The attorney waved his client off and walked toward the stand while asking, "Miss Evans, did you change your name when you married your *second* husband? And didn't he happen to be the attorney you used in your *first* divorce?"

May Shapiro bolted onto her feet and yelled, "I object, your honor!"

Pollack looked at the judge and uneasily explained, "Judge, I want to show the Court that after *two previous* marriages, the plaintiff never showed *any* intention of maintaining a true marriage. A true relationship--"

Falzone banged his gavel and proclaimed, "Objection sustained!" then looked at Pollack and advised, "Counselor, I strongly suggest you find another line of questioning."

Pollack timidly returned to the table and slid more papers around... obviously stalling. Suddenly, he thought of something.

"Miss Meyers, uh...I mean Miss Evans. On the evening you and your husband returned from Hawaii, a trip *you* referred to as 'the honeymoon you never had,' you stated Steve punched you, then threw you against a wall so hard...you couldn't move your right arm. Yet you never tried to leave the house. Was there a reason you didn't leave?"

Ginger coldly replied, knowing she was lying, "He said he'd kill me if I left."

Steve was stunned to hear his wife say those words.

"He threatened to kill you? How?"

"With his gun. Steve had a gun. His grandfather gave it to him. He was a soldier and brought it back from Germany."

"Has your husband ever hit you before?"

It was something she couldn't lie about.

"No."

"Did he ever *threaten* you with his gun, or in *any* manner?"

Ginger looked at her devastated husband and answered, "No."

"Tell the Court what Steve did *after* he supposedly assaulted you."

"He packed for the business trip he was going on the next day, then went to bed," she replied innocently.

"Your sister lives a few blocks away. You were just assaulted. Did you go to her for help once he was asleep?"

Ginger gave a look of uncertainty to her mother, then returned her focus to Pollack and answered, "No."

The Delivery Man saw *the look*…and who it went to.

"Did you call her?" Pollack asked.

"No."

"And the next day, the day Steve left for Cleveland, you went to work, correct?"

"Yes."

"And the following day, correct?"

"Yes."

Pollack was feeling a little better about himself after getting some right answers, so he pressed, "Then on the third day you came to the County Courthouse with an attorney and filed a Restraining Order stating your husband assaulted and threatened you, correct?"

"Correct."

"Why did you wait three days?"

Sadly, *almost* honestly, Ginger showed some emotion when she revealed, "I didn't know what to do. I didn't want to end my marriage."

Only the Delivery Man saw Laura and Francine look at one another upon Ginger's response. That wasn't the answer the two women wanted her to give.

"Did you have your husband's hotel number in Cleveland, or his cell number?" Pollack continued.

"Yes."

"Did you call him to talk about it?"

"No."

"Did he call *you* while he was away?"

Glancing to Laura, Ginger knew she was about to do her mother's bidding, then replied, "Yes. But I let them go to the machine. He'd leave messages as if nothing was wrong."

Unexpectedly, Steve stood and erupted, "That's *a lie!* I called *every day!* We talked *every day!* She *never* said *anything* about something being wrong! Why are you lying, Ginge?"

The judge banged the gavel and ordered Pollack, "Control your client!"

Once Steve calmed enough to sit, Pollack reiterated to Ginger, "You *never* spoke when he called?"

"No."

"Did you keep those messages?"

"No. I deleted them after each call. I didn't want to hear his voice anymore."

Steve was visibly fuming, but knew to keep quiet.

Pollack needed to show his client he was giving it his best shot…before the attorney sold the innocent Steve Meyers down the proverbial rapids without the required paddle.

"Miss Evans, you claimed your injuries were such that you couldn't move your arm, but you still managed to go to work for two days, discuss the matter with an attorney, *not* your husband…and then you and your attorney came to the courthouse to--"

Again, Shapiro stood and yelled, "Objection! My client was *assaulted!* Why *shouldn't* she file a complaint?"

Without letting the defense provide a rebuttal, Judge Falzone again decreed, "Sustained!"

Irving Pollack silently looked down. He knew it was a lost cause.

Laura smiled at the judge. This time he smiled back. The Delivery Man watched the circus that the Meyers-Evans R.O. hearing had become.

Steve sat at the defendant's table…stunned. He looked at Ginger as if he were a wounded puppy and saw an equal twinge of pain and guilt on her face. He knew his mother-and-sister-in-law saw it, too. And though he stared at Ginger…she wouldn't look at him.

Shapiro, Laura and Francine beamed confidently. Tina's glaring at Steve changed to a look of "*I got you!*" as she watched the man who loved her mother fall apart. Tabitha was bored.

And the Delivery Man caught it *all*.

Several minutes later the two attorneys stood at their respective tables ready to state their final arguments in order to sway Judge Falzone's decision. Steve sat still, near tears, as confusion over what had happened enveloped him.

"Your honor," Shapiro started, "The plaintiff asks the bench to reconsider the Temporary Restraining Order and grant a Permanent one against the defendant. We're also alerting the court that Miss Evans has filed divorce proceedings…" She turned, looked at the crushed Steve Meyers and continued, "…with no intention of reconciliation." Turning toward the judge, the attractive attorney smiled and sat next to her client.

Irving Pollack, shaking now more than before knowing he would regret what he was about to say, took a deep breath, then stated, "Your honor, my client believes this entire matter is based on an event that occurred more than three years ago concerning the daughter of Miss Evans, and her boyfriend."

Having already made his decision and not giving a damn what the defense had to say, Falzone looked at Pollack and slammed down his gavel.

"Counselor, seeing as this marriage is headed for divorce, there's no sense in allowing your client to have contact with the plaintiff or access to the marital residence. I'm making the Temporary Order…Permanent. That also includes contact with *any* member of the plaintiff's family." Focusing even harder on Pollack, the judge continued, "I recommend you advise your client of the penalty for doing so. It's this Court's decision that--"

Pollack somehow grew the balls to say, "But your honor, I wasn't finished."

"Yes you were, Counselor. And if you want to be found in contempt, all you need to do is interrupt me or open your mouth one more time."

That was it. Falzone's words put Steve over the edge, causing him to stand and yell, "That's *insane!* What *is* this? A set-up?"

Even the people in the gallery grumbled at what they saw and heard.

Judge Falzone repeatedly banged the gavel and shouted, "Order!"

Pollack returned to his seat…beaten.

The Club wore their victory like a badge of honor.

And the Delivery Man again caught it *all.*

"Bailiff!" barked the judge. "Escort Miss Evans to her car. If she's confronted by the defendant…*throw him in jail!*" Then he finished the hearing with *another* slamming of the gavel and said. "Court is recessed. Thirty minutes."

The Delivery Man couldn't believe what he had just witnessed and shook his head as he watched the judge step from the bench and head toward his chambers.

Steve, now confused more than ever, watched his attorney and friend nervously stuff papers into his briefcase. Pollack made it a point not to look at his client.

Within eight months of Steve Meyers being removed from his townhouse and having been served with divorce papers, he lost his job, his health insurance, his car, access to his possessions and was living in the basement of a friend's home...unable to pay rent.

And he never realized Irving Pollack sold him out.

CHAPTER 6

The Story

It was 9:20AM, on Tuesday, September 26th, 2017, and just another beautiful day in Southern California. Within the Los Angeles FBI offices at 11000 Wilshire Blvd, between Veterans Avenue and South Sepulveda Blvd, young and eager Agent Lester Jordan started the morning maneuvering through the obstacle course of the 16th floor's busy hallway with an armful of twelve thick file folders…in a rush to get them to his boss.

The label on the top folder read, "Sherry Hoffman."

Before knocking on the door that read "ASAC – F. Barrett," Jordan had wisely learned to listen first, to determine the mood of his superior. He found that out the hard way shortly after being assigned to the L.A. field office, but learned quickly.

"This piece…of…*shit!*" was heard a good two feet from the door, followed by an equally loud, "Someone *please* get me a god-damn secretary to do this!"

Sitting at his desk and up-to-his-ass in paperwork was the Serial Homicide Division's Assistant Special Agent in Charge, Fred Barrett, black, 56 years old, and a real "I can't wait to retire next year, but love my job" type. To his subordinates he was known via the acronym, "Asac Barrett."

He also hated computers and believed computers hated him.

Barrett was trying to open an email attachment, but it wasn't doing what he wanted or expected it to do…and it was frustrating him.

That was it.

He had *had* it.

Making a fist and pulling back his arm to punch the thin computer monitor…Barrett realized the futility of it. They'd only replace it with another one.

As he unclenched his hand, Agent Jordan knocked on the door.

"Enter!"

The agent figured he'd start his boss's day off with some good news as he stepped inside.

"Ballistics confirmed it. They're all from the same nine-millimeter."

Barrett wasn't listening. He pointed to the monitor and asked his young subordinate, "You know how to make this thing work?"

Switching gears while still struggling with the folders, Jordan responded, "Depends, sir. What are you trying to do?"

With growing frustration, Barrett answered, "My granddaughter sent me a picture." His voice grew louder as he stared at the screen. "A seven year old can make this fucking thing work. Why won't it work for *me?*" Then louder still, and toward the door. "I want a *god...damn...secretary!*"

Agent Jordan placed the twelve files on the desk's least covered spot and said, "No hiring of new administrative personnel, sir. Budget cuts. You know that." He walked behind the desk, placed the mouse onto the attachment, tapped it, answered a security question and the picture of a young child appeared on the monitor.

Once Barrett saw it, his frustrations disappeared. Smiling and without taking his eyes from the image, he said, "Remind me to put you in for a promotion." After pausing a few seconds, he continued, "But no increase in salary. Budget cuts. You know that." Then he laughed and smacked the desk. The vibration caused the top folder to slide off the new pile, spilling out two graphic photos of Sherry Hoffman's bullet-riddled body surrounded by blood, lilies and shell casings.

Barrett picked one up and eyed it grimly. He soon realized he was holding it next to his granddaughter's image on the monitor, causing an abrupt change in his attitude. He became "the law."

"I'm assigning the case to Valentine. She's the agent for this. Bring these to her office," Barrett ordered as he returned the photos to their folder and handed it to Jordan, then continued, "Tell her this gets the highest priority and I want the bastard responsible...*now.*"

Shortly after leaving Barrett's office, Agent Jordan knocked on the door bearing the nameplate, "Serial Homicide Division – Special Agent – P.L. Valentine."

"Yeah...c'mon in," came from the voice inside.

Jordan had been in Valentine's office several times since being assigned to the L.A. division and always enjoyed being there. The wall to the left of the desk had a corkboard pinned with crime scene photos and the room's only window. On the right wall above a small couch was a stretched-out map of the world. In the corner farthest from the door was a wall-mounted TV, a rack of weights and a treadmill.

But what Jordan liked most were the framed photos and citations adorning the wall behind the desk.

One was a wedding photo of Pai Lee and her husband, Sean Valentine. Anyone seeing it could observe the love in their eyes. Others were of Sean in Marine fatigues and dress uniforms, a few showed the couple at gun ranges, and several were of them romantically holding each other in exotic locations around the world. The citations read, "In gratitude to Special Agent Pai Lee Valentine" from the Director of the FBI and the President of the United States for jobs well done. In the center of it all was a framed Medal of Honor with the inscription, "To Sean Valentine, in recognition of personal acts of valor under enemy fire."

In a high-back leather chair behind the desk sat the woman in the photos reading a report on her computer. She was the one Assistant Special Agent in Charge Barrett confidently entrusted the related 9 millimeter killings to, and the FBI agent Lester Jordan looked up to…Pai Lee Valentine, Chinese, 36 years old, five-foot-seven, and in exceptional muscular and physical shape.

Pai Lee took her eyes off the screen to see the new stack of folders placed on her desk. Raising her eyebrows, she looked at Jordan and asked, "And?"

Still a little nervous in her presence, he repeated what he was told to say.

"Asac Barrett said this gets top priority and he--"

Imitating her boss, Pai Lee eased the tension by finishing the sentence in unison with him, "Wants the bastard responsible…" They both paused for a second and simultaneously ended with, "*Now!*"

Agent Jordan pointed to the stack and said, "Twelve so far. The most recent is on top." He paused a second, then continued, "He said you're 'the agent' for this."

Randomly taking a folder from the middle of the pile, Valentine pulled out an 8x10 glossy to see a dead male in his early 60s sitting at the wheel of a new Corvette. A bullet hole was in the center of his forehead, with eight torso holes that caused blood to cover his lower body and the seat.

With her eyes on the picture, she asked, "Think that's an honor?" Turning the photo toward him, Valentine cynically continued, "You wanna look at this shit day and night?"

He nervously responded, "No sir…uhm, ma'am. But it *does* come with the job."

"So you'd better get used to it," came her sarcastic-but-true reply.

Returning the photo and folder to their original place, Valentine looked at the pile she was now in charge of, then eased back into the leather chair and took a deep breath. Agent Jordan knew it was time to go.

Once he was out the door, she took the top folder, looked at the name and said, "Okay Sherry Hoffman, let's see what you're about."

CHAPTER 7

Because

The high-speed ferry from Hong Kong pulled into the Macau dock at 7:20PM on Wednesday, September 27th. Right on time.

As dozens of passengers disembarked, the dressed-for-business, briefcase-carrying Delivery Man was the last to step off. He took in the evening skyline...a view he had seen nine times and in every season, but tonight he noticed a chill in the early-fall air.

He eyed a nearby building on the shoreline and walked toward it.

Approaching the security gate, he clipped an employee pass onto the lapel of his jacket, complete with his photo and the name "Ralph Pesce," then casually entered the Shun Tak China Travel Ship Management Complex with a smile after the guard checked his credentials.

The Engine Maintenance Facility was the size of a commercial jet hangar...complete with a sprawling concrete floor surrounded by metal walls and a corrugated metal ceiling. Everyone from the day shift was gone. The night crew was skeletal. Standing on a scaffold was the sole worker replacing a bent turbine blade above the large motor suspended by thick, massive chains.

Except for a work-light above the section being repaired, the room was dark. The mechanic laughed and sang along to John Pardi's "Dirt On My Boots" emanating from an iPad next to his tool box...echoing throughout the enormous space.

Gary Pogue was a good-ol'-Texas-boy in his mid-30s. He took the job three weeks earlier after working on small jets in the Dallas area for a few years.

Once he loosened three bolts on the cover above the blades, Gary reached into the tool box, pulled out a shiny flask, unscrewed the top and took a mouthful of whiskey. It wasn't his first of the night.

Hearing footsteps, he replaced the cap on the flask, hid it under some tools, stopped the music and looked around the empty space.

That was when he saw someone walk out of the darkness, barely into the light emitted from above the engine.

Gary called out, "Can I help ya?"

With the briefcase in one of his gloved hands, the Delivery Man looked up, smiled and calmly said, "Yeah, I hope so. I'm looking for Gary Pogue from Carrollton, Texas."

Gary eyed him dubiously. Climbing down the scaffold, he arrogantly asked, "How'd you get in here? This is a secured area."

Just as the slightly drunk mechanic reached the ground, the Delivery Man asked, "Are you Gary Pogue?"

Gary walked to the end of a long metal tool cabinet and leaned an arm on it. The man who asked the question stood on the other end, separated from his target by six feet and a few tools atop the cabinet.

Wanting to sound tough, Gary said, "Yeah, that's me. And maybe you didn't hear me, fella. I said this is a secured--"

"I heard you, *fella*," mimicked the Delivery Man as he casually placed the briefcase on the tool cabinet, opened it and reached inside.

When his gloved hand emerged, Gary was facing the silencer.

Their eyes locked.

Softy and calmly, the Delivery Man asked the stunned mechanic, "Remember Becky? Remember that cute little girl you married about four years ago?"

Trying not to show the fear inside him, Gary threw his shoulders back, cocked his head and answered, "Yeah...so? Who the fuck're *you?* Am I supposed to be *scared-a* you or somethin'?"

As if he didn't hear Gary's words, the Delivery Man continued with what he was saying.

"Right now she's sitting in her mother's piece-of-shit trailer. Alone. Mutilated." Disgust took over the Delivery Man's face, causing his thumb to pull the gun's hammer back two clicks. "Meanwhile, you moved here and got this job. Here, in a place where nobody knows what a piece of shit you are. Now...is that fair, cowboy?"

Gary's adrenaline and whiskey-courage kicked in, so he asked, "What's that got to do with you, asshole?"

The Delivery Man raised his index finger to his lips and whispered, "*Shhhhhh*," then smiled. "I'm here for Becky. For *all* the Beckys. For the people who get fucked by people like you. And that's all you need to know…*asshole*."

Realizing he'd never get another chance, Gary grabbed a long-handled ratchet off the cabinet, stepped toward the intended victim and swung it, hoping to hit whatever he could. With trained precision the Delivery Man effortlessly stepped aside…causing the ratchet to miss by a mile.

Looking at the off-balanced Gary, the Delivery Man pointed his Walther and sorrowfully said, "Becky may not have anything left to give you, but *this*…is from me."

The Delivery Man pulled the trigger and put a hole in the center of his target's throat. Gary grabbed his neck as blood squirted between his fingers. He tried to scream…but no sound came out of his mouth. Only blood.

That was when a second bullet entered Gary's right breast.

As air escaped through the hole in his lung, the badly wounded mechanic staggered and watched the trigger be pulled again. The bullet hit Gary's left breast…exploding in his heart. Before the body dropped like a stone, a single bullet went into the center of Gary's forehead.

Spent shell casings hit the concrete and echoed off the metal walls and ceiling as the Delivery Man silently emptied the 9mm magazine into his victim, then placed the pistol in the briefcase and stepped into the darkness.

Leaving the complex, he once again smiled at the Security Guard, then walked to the dock, showed his ticket and boarded the 8:30PM ferry back to Hong Kong.

By 9:20PM, the Delivery Man was sitting at his favorite table in Caprice, the elegant French restaurant on the 6th floor of Hong Kong's Four Seasons Hotel, still dressed in a suit and tie, ensconced in the surroundings and the view of the Kowloon Peninsula and the brightly lit boats, ferries and ships passing through Victoria Harbor.

With the candle flickering on a table for four, he sat alone appreciating the cellist, pianist and harpist performing The Beatles "Because," and thinking it was the ideal selection for the time and place. The tuxedoed table service catered to his every whim throughout the gourmet meal paired perfectly with the accompanying wine…and he was content with his solitude.

Scanning a few tables over, he happened to eye an American man and woman…happy.

Seeing the look of love in their eyes and embraces, it brought a smile to the Delivery Man. One that came from deep inside. One that evoked memories of a special slice of his life. A happy slice.

He bounced back to reality when a waiter placed the check on the table, then walked away. Taking a billfold from inside his jacket, the Delivery Man removed two one-hundred dollar bills and laid them on the table.

The couple noticed the well-dressed American as he passed their table. He smiled, nodded to them, continued to the door and took the elevator up to his suite.

CHAPTER 8

The 9 Millimeter Case

By the morning of Tuesday, October 3rd, the map on Special Agent Pai Lee Valentine's wall now had nine red stick pins protruding from various locations in North America, and three in Asia. Each was tagged with times and dates...and all within the previous nine months.

Sitting at her desk, Valentine spoke toward the speakerphone as she scanned documents and photos from Sherry Hoffman's file. She did it while simultaneously cleaning a .40 Glock that was spread across her desk in six pieces and in a conversation with her most reliable tech in the Research Department.

"I have a dozen homicides on two continents starting last January. Each shot nine times with the same weapon and with no specific travel pattern in relation to the dates of the events. No witnesses, prints, DNA, robberies, rapes...*nothing.*"

Reassembling the weapon, she smoothly slid the barrel into place as she continued talking.

"After a week of living inside these fucking files, other than each one getting divorced within days to a couple of months prior to their murder, there are threads in these files I'm not finding. I'm thinking the local police may have missed some details, details that never made the files. I need you to get me everything the local law has on each victim. Personal stuff. Gossip. *Anything*...and I need it pronto."

The pistol was now fully assembled.

"I'll email you the file numbers."

Pai Lee slammed a loaded magazine into the grip, thanked the tech, hung up and went back to reading Sherry Hoffman's file as anger and frustration enveloped her face.

The computer's digital clock read 2:27AM, Friday, October 6th, as Valentine studied the "9 Millimeter Case." Finishing with one folder, she'd drop it atop an organized pile on the office floor and would pick up the next one. With each page and photo her eyes went from pain, to anguish, to remorse…to resentment. That she couldn't determine the connective links to each murder angered her more.

The first knock of the day on her door came at 9:12AM. Eleven folders were neatly stacked at her feet as she reviewed, for the fourth time, the document Sherry Hoffman was reading before her flower delivery.

Lifting her head from the paperwork, the Special Agent called out, "Yeah, come in."

She wasn't expecting her boss to enter…especially carrying a cup of coffee and a folder.

Without saying anything, Barrett walked to her desk, put the folder in the center of the now almost-clean space, then handed her the coffee.

Pointing to the folder, he said, "Ronald Gladue. Eight weeks ago. Around midnight…while he was taking a leak in the Men's Room of a South Korean bowling alley. In Seoul. He moved there a few months earlier. That's why it took so long for us to find out about it. Another fuckin' hit in Asia…"

Pai Lee took a mouthful of coffee and waited to hear the common thread.

"…with the same fuckin' gun." Then he looked at her appearance. "Did you sleep last night?"

She pointed to the far wall and answered, "On the couch. About three hours…I think."

Returning Sherry Hoffman's divorce decree to its folder, Valentine looked at the label on the new file and wrote Gladue's name with the time and date of his murder on a small piece of paper. With her coffee in hand, she walked to the map above the couch, pulled a red pin from several others stuck in one corner, then put it through the paper and pinned it into Seoul.

Taking a few steps back and looking at the thirteen pins across two continents, she said, more to herself than to the other person in the room, "Ronald Gladue in Seoul. About 4 weeks earlier it was Sherry Hoffman in Mamaroneck, New York. Five weeks before that it was Susan Martino in Santa Rosa, California. Before that, Alex Barker in Tokyo. Then Eric Gold outside of Bangkok. Four across America…" She closed her eyes and thought for a few seconds, then continued, "Joseph Blum in New Orleans, Tania Butler outside of Des Moines, Duane Griffin in Las Vegas, and Shaunt Romano in West Palm Beach."

Barrett was impressed that she had memorized the names and locations of the victims, and the order they were hit…*in reverse.*

"The first kill in Asia was Kelly Rubin outside a Nepalese ashram. Before that it was the three in America…Stanley Gose in Scottsdale, Valeria Lomax in Brooklyn, and as far as we know, the very first hit on Friday, January twenty-seventh of this year, Theodore Schor, found dead sitting on his tractor in a barn in Newton, Kansas. It took a day or two to thaw him out." Then she slyly smiled and quipped, "I sure hope this shooter's getting frequent flyer miles somewhere."

She walked to her desk and opened Gladue's folder, as if looking for something specific. Seeing what she was hoping to see…a grin crossed her face as she reached for the phone and tapped a few buttons.

Barrett watched her go into action.

Once someone answered, she got down to business.

"It's Valentine. I want a Similarity Report. Credit cards, hotels, cell and video calls, text messages, transportation, visa and passport records, FedEx, UPS and Postal tracking information and anything else pertinent to the dates and locations I'll email you in about thirty minutes." She listened to the voice on the other end, then said, "No. Not Monday. I need it today. Yeah. Hold on."

She hit the phone's Hold button and looked at Barrett.

"The first threads were easy. They were killed with the same gun, the same number of rounds and within several weeks of getting divorced. Now I've got to figure out the relationship between the ex-spouses and the hitter…whoever he or she is."

The ASAC smiled knowing he put the right person on this case. There was nothing he needed to say, so he gave a thumbs-up and left the office. Valentine hit the Hold button and got back to the call.

"Please don't give me any shit. The longer this takes, some recently divorced man or woman could be getting whacked for no good reason other than somebody's pissed off at them." She listened to the caller and sarcastically replied, "Gimme a break, will ya? I've been given Top Priority on this from Barrett. Do *you* want to tell him it'll have to wait until Monday?" Her tone changed with her next reply, "Yeah, I told him I slept for a couple of hours, but I've been up all night and can barely keep my eyes open." After pausing a second, she laughed and said, "And if you make some joke about my eyes, as tired as I am I'll come there and Kung Fu your ass in front of the entire department, white-boy."

She listened for a few more seconds, then calmly answered, "Yes, all night…again." Looking at the pile on the floor, she took a deep breath and said, "Thanks. Keep an eye out for my email."

Pai Lee replaced the receiver to its base, swiveled her chair around and looked at a picture of her husband, then drank more coffee and gave him a wink.

That same day, in a large, neatly appointed room used as an office, the Delivery Man sat comfortably at his desk in a high-rise condo overlooking a metropolis that resembled all the others in North America. He most enjoyed watching the sun reflect off the steel and glass structures…even doing it while he was on a call.

Speaking calmly, cordially and eloquently to the speakerphone, he said, "The equitable distribution offer you're proposing isn't very fair…is it, Counselor?"

The lawyer he was talking to replied, "We think it is."

Holding back a chuckle, the Delivery Man asked, "What would make you think I'd expect *my* client to agree to it?"

The voice coming from the speaker *did* laugh as he answered, "Because they'll fight over it for the next two months…and we can *each* bill them another nine or ten grand. You've seen their financials. They won't miss it."

The Delivery Man's voice became serious as he ever-so-slowly turned his eyes from the view, then glared at the phone and asked, "But if we agree on a logical distribution of assets and property right now, why continue this longer than we need to?"

The sarcastic reply came as, "Are you new to divorce law, Counselor? How long have you been practicing?"

That was it. The Delivery Man knew the kind of lowlife he was speaking to, and let him know it.

"Long enough. That's all you need to know. And if you don't agree to more reasonable terms within the next forty-eight hours, this conversation and your stalling practices will be brought to the attention of your client and the Ethics Committee. Do I make myself clear... *Counselor?*"

Silence came from the speaker, followed by a response that lacked the bravado of his previous comments as the lawyer softly answered, "The papers will be on your desk by end-of-business tomorrow."

The Delivery Man tapped the button on the phone, disconnecting the call. Returning his eyes to the expanse of civilization, he shook his head saying, "And they wonder why people hate lawyers."

CHAPTER 9

Fuck You, Your Honor!

It was Wednesday, October 11th. Special Agent Valentine and Asac Barrett looked like any two business people on their lunch break strolling along The Bluff, the scenic pathway on Ocean Avenue overlooking the Pacific from atop the cliffs of Santa Monica. Even with the beauty and tranquility of an endless blue sky that went to the horizon, Pai Lee couldn't appreciate it because of the wall she had hit with the 9 Millimeter Case.

As they walked, they kept their gaze forward while Pai Lee said what was on her mind, but not loud enough for bystanders or passing joggers to hear.

"A male body popped up in Macau. Recently divorced. He moved from Texas, got a job and three weeks later…same weapon and number of rounds." Then she shook her head in frustration and continued, "But I'm having a problem with my other hunches."

"Such as?" asked Barrett.

"Travel records. There's *nothing*. No related records for *any* of the locations and dates of the hits. Credit cards. Not even calls or texts. What does that sound like to you?"

"It's as if this person either travels *without* ID, or with *multiple* IDs," Barrett ascertained.

"*Exactly*," Valentine quickly replied.

"What else?" he asked.

"The ex-spouses," Valentine frustratingly said in an exhale. "It sounds funny, but based on their locations, demographics, assets, not one of them can be connected to the types of people that would even *know* a hitter… much less the *same* hitter."

Three nannies pushing baby carriages walked toward them, so the conversation stopped until they passed. Valentine turned to make sure they were a fair distance away before continuing.

"These were *revenge* hits. And for five of 'em it meant traveling to another continent to locate and terminate." She stopped walking, causing Barrett to come to a halt and look at her. "Plain and simple, boss...somebody, an unassociated, unrelated third party was pissed off about the way something went down."

"The next step?" her boss asked.

"I just gotta find them. The things that each of these divorces have in common."

"Threads?"

The Special Agent sarcastically answered, "I'll have enough for a friggin' scarf when this is over."

Continuing along the paved path, with fatherly concern Barrett said, "Listen Pai Lee, this person...who*ever* it is...is on a mission. They're smart, and they don't want you changing their plans. I'm putting Agent Jordan on this with you. I want someone to watch your back."

She looked appreciatively at him, then said, "No disrespect, sir, but this one's mine. I'm leaving tomorrow to talk to the ex's. That's where I'll find the next piece. There's a thread there somewhere--"

He cut her off and finished the sentence.

"And you're gonna find it."

Her chest filled with the confidence he provided as they walked. Only now, they took the time to enjoy the view and ocean air.

On that same evening, sitting at his desk admiring the setting sun and enjoying a glass of Aglianico Chianti, the Delivery Man's finger casually tapped his computer-mouse that opened a website showing flags of the fifty states, Washington DC, and the American territories.

Though no one was in the room, he softly said, "Update me, Paula."

The voice of an efficient, well-spoken female who could have been in her late 40's, emanated from the computer's speakers and the flag of Indiana widened to cover the screen.

"Indiana. The Hoosier State. A major provider of America's corn. Home of the Indianapolis Five-Hundred. Indianapolis is the most-populated city in the state. In alphabetical order Indiana is the birthplace of Larry Bird, James Dean, Virgil Grissom, Jimmy Hoffa, Michael Jackson, Eli Lilly, Dan Quayle, Twyla Tharp, Kurt Vonnegut, Jr., Orville and Wilbur Wright--"

No matter how many times he sat through similar lists he always laughed and listened until he couldn't take it any longer.

"Okay, move on. You know what I want."

Within a second the screen changed to Court Hearing Summaries and showed the heading, 'Adams vs Adams – Divorce/Spousal Abuse.' He said, "Tell me."

Paula recited the file's pertinent information.

"On April fifth, two-thousand-sixteen, plaintiff Pamela Adams alleged assault by defendant Charles Adams. A Temporary Restraining Order was issued. The defendant has no previous or similar charges. Evidence submitted showed no visible or medical proof of assault. A Permanent Restraining Order was issued April twenty-first of that same year."

"Yeah, I remember that one." He thought for another second, then smirked, "Aunt Ellie."

Paula continued, "Married for three years, ten months and eight days before plaintiff filed divorce papers two days after the decree of the Permanent Restraining Order. The couple has no children. Plaintiff has refused offers for marriage counseling. The divorce hearing is set for a week from today, Wednesday, October eighteenth, two-thousand-seventeen."

Listening intently, he said, "Print the Restraining Order transcripts. Save and update it as needed and bring it to my attention first thing tomorrow. Then close up shop."

"Yes sir," came the reply, as a printer across the room started printing sheets of text and the Delivery Man walked out of the room holding his glass of wine.

Also on that same evening, a cold early-fall rain pounded the parking lot of a rundown motel on the outskirts of Fort Wayne, Indiana. The heater in the room Charlie Adams was able to afford wasn't working. Sitting on a stained couch, his body shivered under a thin, dirty blanket from the bed. It was apparent Charlie hadn't slept a full night, nor had eaten, shaved or bathed in days.

His hands nervously shook as he tried to take court documents from an envelope, but it was impossible to read through his tears.

Then, Charlie, everyone's friend…a man who had never hurt anyone… collapsed on the floor.

Crying.

Alone.

Near-penniless.

Broken.

At 10:48AM on Thursday, October 12th, Special Agent Valentine disembarked the LAX American Airlines flight into the Dallas-Fort Worth Airport. Once aboard the Hertz van, she pulled a file from her briefcase and programmed the address of a Carrollton trailer park into her phone's GPS. It was standard procedure for agents of *all* law enforcement branches not to use the GPS in rental cars as it leaves a detailed record of their whereabouts.

Valentine's white 2017 Ford Fusion Hybrid silently and slowly drove past trailer homes in conditions that ranged from middle-of-the-road to those that should have been condemned years ago. If there was one that fell between those extremes, it was the trailer the FBI agent's GPS told her to park in front of.

Before knocking on the door, Valentine had a feeling she was going to regret being there.

Genny 'Mama' Stone, an obese woman in a soiled house dress and a multi-colored mess of unkempt hair, swung it open. The immediate stench of stale air, cigarette smoke and three-too-many cats made Valentine want to get back in the car and drive away.

But she didn't.

"C'mon in. Becky's waitin'," said Genny between drags on a cigarette that took smoke into a mouth missing every third tooth, and those that remained were crooked or rotten. "Ya might as well try one more time to git the story outta her. She didn't talk to any *other* po-leece, I doubt she'll talk to y'all. I reckon my girl, she just plain stopped talkin' once-and-fer-all."

The large woman stepped aside and held the door open as far as it would go. Taking the first step, Valentine thought, "If this is what's at the front door, what the hell's gonna be inside?" and tried not to show her reluctance to enter.

But enter she did.

The place was a pig-sty.

Becky Pogue, the catatonic 26 year old ex-wife of Macau murder victim Gary Pogue, was wrapped in a cheap cloth robe, sitting on a stark wooden chair staring out the filthy front window amidst the cluttered, dusty living room.

If Becky didn't look like her world had come to an end and all hope was drained from her being, no one would ever guess she was Genny's daughter. The difference was dramatic. Becky's natural blonde hair, homegrown-beauty and five-foot-four stature were *nothing*. Valentine could see it was the innocence in this gentle child's face. Some would call it *angelic*. There was no deceit within the girl. It was evident to anyone who took the time to look.

Now, Becky's face was hollow. Her eyes gazed longingly into the distance at nothing in particular.

Genny, a cigarette with a two-inch ash hanging between her teeth, popped open a can of beer as the FBI agent looked for the cleanest seat closest to the girl she came to question.

Hitting her phone's Record button, Valentine said, "Becky…I'm FBI Special Agent Pai Lee Valentine. I've been assigned to a case that involves the death of your ex-husband Gary Pogue."

Becky's expression or stare didn't alter.

"I'd like to start by asking if you can give me a reason…*any* reason why someone would want to travel to another country to kill Gary."

There was no reaction. It was as if Becky didn't hear the question.

"Becky…I may be able to find the person who shot him if you tell me what you know."

Genny plopped onto the beer-and-cat-pee-stained couch and said, "I told her you was comin'. Days ago I told her. But she ain't talked. Not a word. Nothin'. Not since the po-leece told her they heard from the China po-leece he was dead. You know, that Pogue-boy, he left her…he left her high, dry 'n *dee-vorced*. Then he moved to wherever that place is and got shot. Po-leece come here fer days. Asked her the same damn questions over and over and over. And they all told her the same bullshit, sayin' *they* was gonna find who killed the bastard."

Though Mama didn't know it, interrupting the Special Agent during an interrogation wasn't something she should have done. Taking her eyes from Becky, Valentine glared at Genny and viciously barked, "I don't give a fuck *what* your local yahoos said! *I'm* the only one who'll find his killer, and if Becky wants to see justice served…" The anger suddenly left her voice as she turned to Becky and gently finished, "…then she needs to speak to me."

After several seconds of silence, and to the surprise of Genny and Pai Lee, Becky turned her eyes from the window, rose from the chair and stood in front of the seated Valentine, separated by only inches. The girl who had been silent for weeks looked down and softly, almost childlike, said, "Justice *was* served, ma'am. Gary's dead."

Hearing Becky shocked her mother to the point of making her speechless and unable to bring the beer can up to her mouth.

Still looking at the woman who traveled to question her, Becky kept speaking, but in short bursts of words and sentences.

"I loved Gary. And when you're in love…you do things for the…*other* person. Things…so they can be happy. So the *two* of you can be…happy."

With her waist even with Valentine's face, Becky untied and opened her cloth robe. Pai Lee raised her head to see the young woman expose two terribly disfigured and horrifically scarred breasts. The nipple was missing from her right one.

Wincing at the sudden and unexpected sight, Valentine quickly diverted her eyes up to Becky's face. Genny turned away and began sobbing.

Becky began her story.

"About two years ago he took me…Gary took me to some doctor. He met him in that strip club he use-ta go to. He had me put two big fake boobs in…in my body. Big ones. *Big*. Like forties. He wanted me to dance. To be a dancer. He said I'd make money. A *lot* of money. Enough money so we could…we could hook our trailer up to his truck. We was gonna move…to Las Vegas. He said I was gonna make a lotta money there…and we'd buy a house. I wanted to…to make my husband happy. That's all."

Becky's face turned sadder than it already was.

"Pretty soon after, they started leakin'. They weren't put in right. Gary said I hadta have 'em cut out right away...or I would-a died." Hearing her daughter say those words caused Genny's crying to get louder. Turning toward her, Becky said, "I'm sorry, Mama. Please don't cry." It didn't help. Seeing her daughter's body mutilated in that way was too much for Genny.

Then the once-angelic face with eyes filled with tears looked at Valentine and continued, "So...he made me go back. Back to the same guy. The same guy who put 'em in...to take 'em out."

Becky's eyes went from Valentine to her own torso and said, "He scarred me up bad." That was when her eyes released the tears she had tried so hard not to let run down her face. It also made the telling of her story harder.

"Once Gary saw me...after I healed. After he saw me like this...he called the po-leece. He said...he said I got drunk. Got drunk and shot at 'im...with his own shotgun. He said I...wanted to kill 'im." She shook her head and wept, "He got a 'Strainin' Order. A 'Strainin' Order so I couldn't go back to our trailer. To our home."

That was when Genny, with venom in her voice, cried, "Then the little shit emptied their bank account and filed fer divorce. She got dee-pressed, missed days at work and lost her job at the market...and without any money or no insurance, my girl couldn't git no doctor or lawyer worth spit." Regaining a bit of composure, the mother went on. "Now she sits here all day and night...lookin' out that window..." She pointed to her daughter's exposed body and cried, "...and lookin' like *that* the rest-a her life."

Becky saw the pain across the FBI agent's face and said, "Justice, Miss FBI-lady?" Trying to hold back more tears, she continued with determination, "Only thing I regret...is not bein' able to...not bein' able to *thank* whoever it was...that *gimme* my justice. *That's* what I'm lookin' fer out this window. I'm waitin' fer that person. *Whoever* it is. I'm waitin' fer 'em to find me. Find me so I can thank 'em *personally*." Then the young woman retied her robe, sat back down, turned to the dirty window and gazed into the distance. She was done talking.

Holding back tears of her own, Pai Lee was quick to see the only thing Becky could be guilty of was putting her love and trust in someone she shouldn't have. She simply couldn't tell the good guys from the bad.

There was no connection to Gary's killer here.

The agent's work was done. Turning off the recorder, she heard the sound of a TV show. Taking her eyes off Becky, Valentine turned to see Genny still planted on the sofa, now surrounded by four cats, drinking beer, smoking another cigarette and tapping on two TV remote controls taped together that were aimed at two dust-covered wooden-enclosed TVs from the 1990s, one atop the other.

Anticipating the Special Agent's question, Genny pointed to one remote and said, "This-un's fer the TV on top. That one has a picture…but no sound." Then she pointed to the second remote, but before she could continue, Valentine said, "Let me guess. The lower one gets sound but no picture."

"Damn, you FBI folks really *are* smart!" yelled Genny, amazed the "big city girl" caught on so quickly.

Not wanting to stick around, the big city girl made her intentions clear.

"Yeah, well…I gotta go. Nice meeting you, and if I need any information, I'll call."

Special Agent Valentine left the trailer as fast as she could, got in her car and sped to the DFW Airport Hilton. Once in her room, she stripped off her clothes, then took a shower and washed her hair. By one o'clock and in fresh attire, she called the Valet to have the clothes she had worn earlier that day dry-cleaned…then turned on the computer to write her report.

The voice from Pai Lee's GPS brought her from the Seattle-Tacoma Airport to a location 18 miles away. Once in the parking lot of her destination, she opened Ronald Gladue's file and took out a photo of a smartly-dressed attractive woman that could be anyone's favorite aunt. No more than five-foot-seven, she was a brunette with brown eyes and a smile filled with happiness. Valentine tapped 'Record' on the phone and started talking.

"Tuesday, October seventeenth, two-twenty in the afternoon. I'm at the nursing home where Anita Gladue now resides. Her doctor said she sleeps most of the day due to her medication, but if she *is* cognizant, I shouldn't expect more than a few minutes before she won't speak about what happened." She paused for a few seconds to think, then continued,

"As of today I will have seen six ex-spouses in six days…women and men with similar stories of lawyers, judges, money, homes, possessions. But these people were hurt most by the love and trust they gave. What the hell did they *go through* to get them to this condition? There's another thread."

It was time for her to find out.

After getting through the receptionist's sign-in paperwork, Valentine was led to Anita's room, and was once again startled by what she saw. Sitting on the side of the bed waiting to go for a walk was Ronnie Gladue's ex-spouse. Though Anita was only 41, her hair had turned nearly all white, and there were dark, heavy bags beneath once youthful eyes that would never be the same again. She needed the support of a cane to walk, and clothes that used to fit perfectly now hung on a body that no longer seemed to care.

Anita extended a weak hand to the FBI agent as they shook during introductions.

From a third story window, Anita's doctor watched his patient and the FBI agent walk the path in the Meditation Garden. He was hoping Valentine would open some inner door that could lead toward Anita's recovery.

The women slowly strolled through the flowers, and though the doctor couldn't hear what was being discussed, the visual was easy to follow.

After a few minutes, Anita struggled to answer a question, then her face turned sad. *Very* sad. The patient stopped walking and began to shake. Valentine gently took Anita's shoulders and tried to calm her down. It wasn't working. The two women locked eyes. Anita couldn't hold her emotions back any longer and burst hysterically into tears. All Pai Lee could do was hug her…tightly.

Over the last few days it had become normal for Valentine to sit in rental cars and weep for the damaged, innocent people she had to interview because of the related murders in the 9 Millimeter Case. She felt more pity for *these* victims than for the ones who were murdered.

Looking frazzled, she again opened Gladue's file and hit Record on the phone.

"It's two-fifty-five and I just left Anita Gladue, Ronnie-the-bowler's ex-wife. The same M.O. as the others. In this case, Ronnie took out the

Restraining Order, somehow sucked up her personal investments and assets, and had her removed from the house she inherited from her family, then he won it in the divorce. He sold it literally a day later and took off for South Korea once the check cleared. Why Korea? The Army. He was stationed there for a couple of years. Six years ago he met Anita. They married after dating for more than a year. Then, three-and-a-half years later he wiped her out…emotionally and financially. And that's *another* thread."

She looked at a separate piece of paper on the passenger seat and kept going.

"So far, each ex-spouse, in some way…was a victim. Each relationship and resulting divorce ended in a mental meltdown. It's like some kind of a 'related conspiracy' by 'unrelated people.' Very weird. *Very* weird. But how are they connected to the killer? *That's* what I've got to find out."

She turned off the recorder, put the file in her briefcase, started the car and gave a sigh, "Tomorrow…Scottsdale. Thursday…West Palm Beach. Friday…New York. Saturday…home."

It was a nice day in mid-October for everyone in the Fort Wayne area, except for Charles Adams who had spent that morning in the Allen County Courthouse.

Once again, Judge Mahoney sat on the bench before the Indiana state flag. He looked at the audience of two dozen from his high-back chair, most of them not paying attention to the case going on because they had their *own* problems…except for the Delivery Man, who sat center aisle on the defendant's side "watching the show," as he referred to it.

Sitting at the defendant's table was a noticeably malnourished, disheveled, distraught Charlie with his inept, bargain-basement attorney.

At the plaintiff's table sat the well-attired and joyously happy Pamela Adams next to her matching prosecuting attorney. In the row behind the bar sat Rick and Aunt Eleanor.

The Delivery Man watched *them* as much as he observed the court proceedings.

Banging the gavel, the judge shuffled some paperwork and got down to business.

"Let the record show on this day, October eighteenth, two-thousand-seventeen, the marriage between Pamela Adams and Charles Adams has been terminated in divorce." The Delivery Man watched the judge's eyes scan Eleanor, who provided her usual sly-smile and wink. Knowing he'd be getting blown in his chambers at lunchtime, Mahoney reviewed a piece of paper, then continued, "Also let the record show the Equitable Distribution Agreement, determined by this court to be fair and just--"

"You call giving it *all* to her is '*equitable*'? What fucking planet do *you* live on, judge?" came from Charlie, who stood and yelled with what little energy and self-pride he had left.

The attorney grabbed Charlie's arm, more to show the judge he was trying to control his client and save his *own* ass.

Mahoney roared, "Be quiet, Mr. Adams!"

Charlie puffed out his chest as best he could through his soiled, wrinkled clothes and said, "Or *what?* You'll throw me in jail again? You *might as well!* I got fired 'cause I couldn't think straight and do my job. You took away my home over a bullshit Restraining Order and gave it to *her*. Everything I owned. Every semblance of my life. You gave it away! All I've got left are garbage bags filled with filthy clothes." He raised his two middle fingers to the figure of authority and justice and yelled, "Send me to jail! Big fucking deal!"

The silence in the courtroom was immediate. Every set of eyes were now on the frail man sure to be sent to the dungeon and wouldn't see daylight until he was dragged to the gallows.

Mahoney slammed the gavel, causing everyone to turn to the bench, awaiting the axe to fall on the poor defendant.

The expected response didn't happen. The judge smiled, but there was a sly twinge to it. He spoke at a normal volume, though made sure all ears heard him...especially Eleanor's.

"No, Mr. Adams. You'll leave this courthouse through the front doors today and survive like everyone else." Then his demeanor changed when he warned, "But let me remind you...there is still a Restraining Order against you. Should you violate it, you'll certainly be going to--"

"Fuck you, your honor!" came from the defendant, followed by cheers from the gallery and laughter from the Delivery Man. Then Charlie turned to his attorney and forcefully articulated, "And fuck you, too...you mute, worthless piece of shit!" The cheers, laughter and applause swelled.

The Delivery Man couldn't help but be amused at the chaos.

Mahoney banged the gavel so hard and repeatedly that it broke, causing him to yell, "Bailiff! Bailiff! Either shoot that man or get him out of my courtroom...*now!* Let the record show this case has been resolved!"

As the gallery calmed down, two Court Officers rushed to the now-single Charles Adams, grabbed his weak arms and forcefully led him out of the well and through the bar. As he was being roughly ushered past the Delivery Man, the two men caught each other's eyes. Somehow, Charlie sensed the stranger felt his pain.

The officers led Charlie out of the courtroom, down the marble staircase and through the front doors of the courthouse before releasing their grips.

Charlie Adams was now alone. Completely alone. Homeless. Penniless. And he *still* didn't understand what had happened over the last nineteen months of his life.

A REMINDER

"To understand the meaning of one story,
you must often know the details of several others."

Italian Proverb

CHAPTER 10

Don't Get Mad…Get Glad

Two days after Charlie and Pamela Adams' divorce, the weather in Fort Wayne was still exceptional.

No one noticed the rented SUV, or the Delivery Man in a suit, parked across the street from the home that now had Pamela's name on the deed. He had been sitting there all of ten minutes when the large garage door opened and Rick, in a black Lexus RC, pulled out and drove away. Then the garage door closed.

The Delivery Man's fingers tapped a button on a small electronic device. Red digital letters flashed, "Received & Recorded." He lifted his head to make sure the Lexus was gone, then tapped another button on the devise. Green letters flashed "Transmit," and the garage door opened. Carrying a satchel, he stepped from the SUV and nonchalantly walked toward the open garage door with the Lincoln MKZ parked on one side.

Once inside, he donned thin black leather gloves, went to the back wall and tapped the button, causing the door to go down. When it closed, he tapped it again. As the door rose to halfway, he re-tapped it…causing it to go down. As it reached the bottom, he tapped the button again, raising it halfway, and then again…closing it.

That was when he heard footsteps approach the interior door from within the house.

The door swung open and Pamela, in a robe and slippers, barked, "Rick! What the hell are you doing?" Once she saw the man in the tailored suit and leather gloves, she yelled "Who the hell are *you?*"

He grinned and calmly answered, "Good morning, Miss Adams. I'm the Director of Sanitation for this part of town. We received a complaint about the way you've been using your garbage bags."

Stunned at the intrusion and unsure of what he was referring to, she asked, "What are you talking about? How did you get in my garage? Where's your ID?"

"Oh, I'm sorry. It's in here," he politely replied as he reached in the satchel. When his hand emerged, it was holding his 9mm with the silencer attached…and pointing at her.

She froze and was only able to utter, "Oh my god."

The Delivery Man shut the house door behind her, then put his index finger to his lips and calmly said to the frightened, shaking divorcee in the cute robe, "*Shhhhh.* There's no need to get nervous. I just want to talk to you about how you throw things away."

Pamela tried, yet was unsuccessful in forming a cohesive sentence and could only stutter, "I…I don't…don't…please don't…"

He again reached into the satchel, this time revealing a roll of duct-tape and a box of extra-large plastic trash bags. Ripping off a foot-long piece of tape, he held it out and said, "I want you to put this over your mouth so I don't have to hear you babble…okay?"

The still-shaking woman nervously nodded, then took the tape and pressed it over her mouth, from ear to ear. Tears began to run down her face and over the tape.

With the gun still aimed at her, the Delivery Man opened the box of trash bags, took two out and handed her one.

"Now step into this," he ordered. Responding to the confused look on her face, he caustically said, "We're doing a test to see how strong they are."

She *wanted* to look at him like he was crazy…but she also wanted to come out of this alive. Pamela took the bag, but her hands were shaking too much to open it.

"Relax, Miss Adams. This won't take long."

She opened the extra-large plastic bag, apprehensively stepped inside and held it up to her waist with both hands. With her mouth taped and through fear-filled eyes she looked at him…waiting for what would come next.

He held up the second bag and said, "Now, I'm going to put this one over you."

Her eyes, though crying, went as wide as they could. Frozen in fear, her head dropped and slowly shook side-to-side. That was when she felt the silencer's barrel against her face.

"Amuse me" were the last words she heard before the large bag was put over her head and hung down to her torso.

Once Pamela was covered, the Delivery Man laid down the gun, then ripped off a long length of tape and wrapped it around her as muffled crying came from inside. It took several long strips of tape to secure the two bags and Pamela's limbs, and throughout it all, her weeping never stopped. Then…she lost her balance and fell onto the concrete floor. What the Delivery Man didn't know was that his victim was writhing in the same place she had laid Charlie's trash bags filled with clothes.

It was time to get his point across.

"Pam…I want you to listen to me."

The giant duct-taped trash bag stopped moving. He returned the roll of tape and box of bags into the satchel and picked up his gun.

"How's it feel to be in a trash bag?" he asked without emotion.

There was only silence, separated by short bursts of crying.

"I asked…how does it feel?"

Now it was just silence.

"Oh!" he laughed. "It's the tape! I forgot. I won't ask any more question, okay?"

The top bag quietly nodded.

"I want you to think of something, okay?"

It nodded again.

"Your whole life is within the walls of a house. A beautiful house. And one day, without knowing why…you can't go home anymore. Then, someone takes what *they* decide you should have and stuffs it in trash bags…and they keep *everything else* because they have someone connected to a judge who can make that happen. Can you imagine what that must feel like? Can you imagine what that can do to a person?" Again he remembers, "Oh, I said I wasn't going to ask you anymore questions. Sorry."

Pamela sobbed. It was all she could do.

"But I want you to think about how that must have felt, okay?"

She nodded again, but this time her sobs sounded more like gasping.

"Is it stuffy in there, Pam?"

The bag nodded frantically.

"Did you think about what I told you?

She nodded, but now weakly.

"Want me to make some air holes for you?"

The bag barely moved.

"The plastic bags and tape are from Charlie. *This*…is from me."

He lowered his pistol and fired a bullet into Pamela's head. Her body kicked back. Then he emptied the magazine into the life-size trash bag.

Returning the gun to the satchel, he tapped the button on the wall, raising the garage door. Removing his gloves, he walked across the street to the SUV and pressed a button on the electronic device. The green letters flashed "Transmit," closing the garage door.

He pulled away listening to Bob Dylan's "Like A Rolling Stone."

CHAPTER 11

A Hitter With A Conscience?

At the same moment Pamela Adams was being turned into a leaky trash bag, Pai Lee Valentine was driving from New York City's LaGuardia Airport to Mark Hoffman's White Plains apartment. Having seen eight ex-spouses, she no longer thought about what to ask or expect. It was causing her to arrive at the interrogations without the hardened appearance of a tough FBI agent.

Instead, while driving north she listened to The Beatles channel on the rental's satellite radio. She preferred listening to them just to take her mind off of what she knew she'd be seeing upon meeting the next ex-spouse.

A short time later she was once again holding an open file and speaking into her recorder while sitting on another third-hand couch, this time in Sherry Hoffman's ex-husband's sparsely furnished studio apartment.

Mark, 46 years old, drained of life, was on the edge of despair as his hands unconsciously rubbed the arms of the old wooden chair he was sitting in.

"Mr. Hoffman, it says here you owned a pharmacy in town, but you lost it. How?" was Valentine's first question after their introductions.

"I don't really know. One day, everything's fine. Then all of a sudden... nothing's the same." As soon as he said it...his thoughts began to drift. "It was a regular day. Nothing special. Then these policemen came in, and in front of everyone, my customers, my friends, the employees.....they handcuffed me. I had no idea why. They said...in front of *everyone*, that I assaulted my wife. Sherry said I beat her up." With the most innocent and sincere look since Valentine was in front of Becky Pogue, Mark broke into tears and cried, "I never hit my wife, Miss Valentine. I loved her. I didn't understand what was happening. I *still* don't know what the hell happened."

Holding back any personal thoughts, words or emotions, Valentine asked, "What can you tell me about the Restraining Order hearing?"

Leaning back in his chair, Mark did his best to compose himself, though his hands began tapping the chair's arms as he told his story.

"I found the best lawyer I could. Sherry told the judge I hit her... *bad*. She didn't have a doctor's report, x-rays...*nothing*. She got up there and cried...said we fought all the time because she told me she wanted a divorce. She told them I said I'd kill her. That's a *lie!* We *never* talked about a divorce. We were happy. I *loved her*. That's why, when the police showed up...I had no idea what they were talking about. I *loved* her. Her and her goddamn lilies." That was when his tears again fell. "And she said she loved *me*."

"What did your lawyer do, Mr. Hoffman?"

His response was quick. It required no thought. It was a sad scene he relived in his mind countless times. Through his nervous hand-tapping and sobbing he replied, "It didn't seem to matter. The judge said since we were going to be divorced anyway, and since Sherry didn't work...I had to find a place to live and I had to pay the mortgage on the house so she could live there, her health and car insurance, and the payments on her car." Mark's face showed the mind-and-heart-stabbing-pain of each memory as he continued, "A small town like this...it didn't take long for it to get around that I was arrested for assaulting and threatening my wife's... even though it *wasn't true*." The hand-tapping became louder and harder. "Nobody cared about the truth. People stopped coming in. I was having trouble keeping up the payments for the house mortgage, the pharmacy's mortgage, my vendors, salaries, this shitty apartment, insurance payments, the cars, my lawyer, *her* lawyer..." He unknowingly started to slam his hands on the arms as he went on. "By the time we got to the divorce three months ago, I was practically broke. Next thing I knew...I lost *everything*. My wife. My business. My house. And then..." His bloodshot eyes pierced into Special Agent Valentine as he woefully uttered, "...I lost my mind."

It was time for the FBI agent to ask the next question...but she couldn't help feeling she was face-to-face with another innocent victim of a system that someone knew how to use against them.

Mark suddenly realized what he was doing to the chair and forced himself to stop. That was when Valentine noticed the palm of each of his hands were red and blistered from sitting for months and hitting the arms of that chair.

"I just don't know what happened, Miss Valentine…or why."

As tears ran down his weary face, all the interrogator could do was watch.

Fred Barrett was at his desk looking at the computer keyboard, frustrated. Agent Jordan sat to the side watching the two people he respected most. Knowing what she was going to show her boss was more important than what he was trying to type, Special Agent Valentine laid photographs of the murder victims across the keyboard. Barrett had no option but to move his hands and look at them.

"There's no doubt about it, sir. Somebody felt they deserved to die."

His eyes rose from the pictures to look at her and sarcastically say, "No shit. Anything else?"

"Yeah," she answered smugly. "After this case, I'll never get married again."

Turning fatherly, he imparted, "Don't say that, Pai Lee. Someday."

She ignored his statement and stayed on track, stating, "Kids. None of these marriages had kids."

"A hitter with a conscience?" questioned the superior.

"Maybe. But without kids, the divorce process moves a lot quicker," then she pointed to the photos. "Those people knew what they were doing. They, or someone close to them, had a plan and knew how to make it work."

"Why just in America and Asia?" he probed.

"No idea yet."

"Keep going," Barrett pressed.

"They all came up as average citizens with no connections to one another in any way. But here's the interesting thing…after looking into each murder victim and their ex-spouse, it was the dead one that used the law to have their spouses removed from their homes, and I mean *quickly* removed, and always by saying they were assaulted or threatened." She needed to take a breath, then kept going. "Granted, I know everyone's capable of killing, but the people I met…they--"

"You're looking for a thread here, right?" Barrett asked as he handed her the photos so he could return to what he was doing.

"*A* thread? Remember I told you I'd have enough for a scarf? Fuck that. Make it a sweater." She gave a small laugh, then went on. "All the ex's were falsely charged with some level of Domestic Violence or Spousal Abuse. The law statistically protects the plaintiff in these matters. In our case, it appears that once the defendants got to court, proving their innocence was next to impossible. And once a weapon or a threat was mentioned, they rarely stood a chance…if at all."

Agent Jordan watched her with admiration as she angrily continued.

"They were ordered to leave their homes, with most having to continue paying for the spouse that set-'em-up to live there. There had to be *some* foul play on the part of an attorney or a judge, or both. And none of *them* can be connected to any nine-millimeter victim or case other than those they were a part of. You know…if we were one of those fucked over by these people, we'd momentarily consider shooting them ourselves."

Barrett stopped his two-finger typing, crossly eyed her and barked, "What are you saying? You condone these hits?" He turned to Agent Jordan and ordered, "You didn't hear *any* of that! Wipe what you just heard Special Agent Valentine say from your memory. That's an order."

Jordan smiled, saluted and said, "Yes sir."

Barrett returned his eyes to Pai Lee and continued, "It's murder, Valentine. It's repetitive, and it's your job to find the person responsible and arrest them!"

Not leaving it to rest, she countered with, "I'm just saying that in *this case* the victims had it coming to them. I'm not saying it was right to kill them, but these people destroyed the lives, *the reason to exist* of those who trusted them the most…and *somebody* settled the score. *That's* all I'm saying."

Her superior took a deep breath, accepted the answer and reluctantly started typing while continuing the conversation with, "What about the hitter with the nine-millimeter?"

Ignoring his question and staying on *her* subject, Valentine said, "Another statement made by each ex was that their marriage wasn't having any problems…at least not as far as *they* knew."

Agent Jordan was following Valentine's details as Barrett again asked, "The hitter?"

Valentine was on a roll and didn't deviate.

"Not one of the victims made an attempt at, or were even *open to*, reconciling. Statistically, that's off the chart."

"Pai Lee! *The hitter!*" he snapped.

"*The bullshit Spousal Abuse and Assault charges, boss! That's* the thread I'm trying to explain to you! One way to narrow down the hitter is by seeing how those bullshit-charges tie into whomever it might be."

That was when Barrett's computer gave a beep and showed an Error message...then the screen went blank.

Valentine gathered her files and sarcastically said, "You know what you need? You need a secretary," as she left the office.

Even with the door closed behind her she heard her superior yell, "*God damn it!* Jordan...get over here!"

She clutched the files and walked the corridors deep in thought. It was only a moment before she was in front of a large framed glass along the wall with American flags draped on the left and right of it. Etched in the glass were the words, "In Memory Of FBI Agents Killed In The Line Of Duty" and lined with names and dates.

Pai Lee laid her fingers on a specific one. A place she had positioned them many times before. Her eyes filled with tears as she looked at the etched words, "Special Agent Sean Valentine — 1979-2015," and whispered, "Thank you for making ours one of the good ones, Sean." Looking around to make sure she was alone, Valentine placed her head against the glass and cried, "But...it's lonely. It's lonely."

CHAPTER 12

Would You Like Miles With That?

The clock on the computer showed there were only three hours left before sunrise. Hunched over the 9 Millimeter folders, Valentine realized the size of each had tripled since the case was put on her desk four weeks earlier.

Legal documents, photos of the murdered victims and pages of handwritten notes were scattered everywhere. She knew the case was getting to her a few days earlier when she started talking to herself.

Reaching for a file, she rambled, "Whoever you are…you're certainly hittin' the right people, I'll give you that. I just hope I get to meet you before I have to shoot you," then slipped out several documents, took one and began reading.

The Special Agent was on the way to her Marina del Rey condo with hopes of crawling into bed for a few hours before returning to the office to find her killer…as the Delivery Man stepped from a Mercedes limo at O'Hare Airport's American Airlines Terminal and took his suitcase and briefcase from the driver. Casually walking inside to the First Class counter, he presented his bag and identification.

Looking at a driver's license with the Delivery Man's photo, the name "Michael Mullins" and an address in "Clearwater, Florida," the customer service rep said, "Good morning, Mr. Mullins. Your final destination today?"

Without missing a beat the traveler replied, "Jacksonville."

While processing what needed to be done, the rep said, "I notice you're not a member of our mileage club. Would you like me to sign you up?"

Giving a friendly smile, Mike Mullins answered, "No thanks. I don't fly much," as he took the stapled baggage-claim and boarding pass, then headed toward the gates.

Two days later the same scene was replayed between the Delivery Man and an Asian woman at the Air China International First Class counter in Beijing. It was an unusually brisk 49 degrees when he entered the terminal, so he was visibly cold as he handed over his passport and ID.

"Good afternoon, sir. And how are you today?" she asked with the customary smile.

He came back with, "Looking to get warm."

Eyeing a passport that displayed "George Gerard" of "Batavia, Illinois," she said, "Let's see, Mr. Gerard," then tapped a few keys and read from the screen, "You're on our three-fifteen to Bangkok. That should be a little warmer for you."

Noticing something as she re-checked the screen, she politely solicited, "Mr. Gerard, I see you're not a member of our mileage club. Would you like me to--"

He cordially shut her down with, "No thanks. I'm not much of a traveler," which left her confused, seeing as he had just come from Illinois and was now headed to Thailand. "That's a lot of miles he's missing out on," the rep thought, but more customers were lining up and she didn't have time to discuss it.

Handing over his passport, ID and boarding pass, she smiled, "There you go. Just take these to the Customs area, and have a nice flight."

And that was exactly what he did.

Late the next afternoon at the Hertz Rental Terminal outside of Louis Armstrong International Airport in New Orleans, the young rental agent handed the Delivery Man keys to an SUV and asked, "Would you like to sign up for our Rewards Prog--"

"No thanks," came from the smiling and dressed-for-business trekker.

Accepting the response, the agent returned the smile and finished his job.

"Thank you for choosing Hertz, Mr. Booth."

Mr. Booth nodded, turned, and with his suitcase in tow, went to his next rented vehicle.

While the Delivery Man was in Louisiana, Special Agent Valentine was stepping into Barrett's office...and wasn't too happy with what she saw. He was sitting at the desk and looked angry. Actually, more pissed off than angry.

A black cloth covered his computer monitor.

She sat in front of the desk and cynically asked, "So? What happened?"

He turned the screen around and removed the cloth. Barrett's keyboard was sticking out of it.

Sarcastically shaking her head and holding back laughter, she stated, "It was just a matter of time."

Rising and walking away from the electronic carnage, her boss got down to business.

"Never mind that. We had to put a lid on some local media a couple of days ago in Indiana about a 'serial killer' when they found that woman wrapped in garbage bags...and I'm catching shit." He took a deep breath. Pai Lee realized the amount of stress he was under when he asked what she already knew was coming, "We've got bodies popping up all over the place. It's October twenty-seventh...almost five fucking weeks since we got this case and I'm getting asked how close you are. So...what do you have?"

Knowing he wanted a straight answer, she gave it to him.

"I've got a person of unknown gender that travels between two continents without a trace. The primary things the murders have in common are...each victim was recently divorced, they were real bitches-or-pricks, and they were all killed with the same weapon. None of the car rental companies show GPS records with addresses of the hits. There's no pattern of where this person will turn up next or what they may...even... look..." She slowed her speech as her mind began racing. "...like."

Something made the proverbial light above her head turn on.

She snapped her fingers and shouted, "I got it! Gotta go!"

Bolting from the office and leaving behind a confused superior, she yelled to anyone who could hear, "Someone *please* get Mr. Barrett a god-damn secretary!" and closed the door behind her.

Wearing sweatpants and a T-shirt while walking on the treadmill in her office, Valentine held fifteen pound weights in each hand as she perspired and spoke into a phone headset giving orders to Agent Jordan. She was onto something and wanted it done *now.*

"I don't give a fuck. Contact the courthouses. We're the *FB-fuckin'-I!* Subpoena them if you have to. I want copies of every security disk and file for those appearances, and I don't want any shit about it. I want them *yesterday!* Over."

While still walking, she dropped the weights to the floor with a thud on each side of the treadmill, much to the anger of whoever was in the office below her, then disconnected the call, stopped the machine and looked at the folders around the room.

With a renewed confidence, she grinned and chuckled, "If this works… I'll get you."

It was a peaceful night with the usual view from the Delivery Man's high-rise condo. The office lights were out. Sitting at the desk with his feet raised and enjoying a snifter of his favorite cognac, the killer Valentine was looking for scanned the computer monitor…the room's only source of light.

"…which was when the defendant was removed from the marital residence," came from Paula's relaxing tones. "The defendant has no prior complaints and has pled Not Guilty. The plaintiff presented no evidence of abuse. A Permanent Restraining Order was placed on the defendant. The day after the R.O. was issued, the plaintiff filed for divorce. All offers of reconciliation from the defendant have not been accepted."

"Put a check on this one and bring all updates to my attention tomorrow." Releasing a frustrated breath, he kept going. "Next?"

"Tomorrow?" the voice unexpectedly probed. "Sunday? You mentioned you wanted to relax for a few days after being gone so long."

"I won't work all day. I promise. You can shut everything down by noon, okay?"

There was silence.

"C'mon, Paula. Noon. *Please?*" he begged, holding back laughter.

"Noon. No later," she gave in.

"Good. Next?"

The screen changed to a new one filled with statistics. Paula reported, "I've compiled the data you requested nine-minutes and twenty-two seconds ago."

"What took so long?" he joked, lifting the snifter to inhale while reviewing the screen.

"Over the past fifteen years, Spousal Abuse cases have increased by six-hundred-and-seven-point-five-two percent. In ninety-three-point-two-one percent of *those* cases, the defendant was found Guilty. In eighty-six-point-one percent of *those* cases, weapon charges or a threat to the plaintiff's life, family, home or workplace were claimed. In appeal, eighty-three-point-six-one percent of the weapon and threat charges, the defendants were found Not Guilty."

"Thank you. Next?"

"I'm still gathering reports and statistics regarding any increase or decrease of homicides and suicides of attorneys over the same period. There seems to be conflicting data, depending on the source."

Drinking his cognac, the Delivery Man scornfully uttered, "I doubt the Bar wants people to know how many lawyers get whacked every year by pissed off clients. Those numbers would probably scare the shit out of a lot of attorneys, too."

The voice humorously responded, "Now there's an image I'd rather not have in my memory files. Thank you for ruining my day."

Instead of laughing, his eyes focused on the details of one of the charts on the monitor.

"Is there anything else I can assist you with this evening, sir?"

His eyes didn't leave the screen and he didn't reply. He was studying the facts about false Spousal Abuse cases and a string of spikes in lawyers that have handled more than their usual share of them.

"Sir?"

He stared deeper at the chart.

"Sir? I know you're there. I can hear you breathing. Testing…one, two, three."

Her words were enough to break his concentration, so he ordered Paula to, "Get me the rest of the data on those attorneys and have it in the morning. Use whatever clearance level you have to provide…if at all."

"Is this a company operation I'm not aware of, sir?"

"Nope."

"Is there anything else tonight, sir?"

"Nope. Close up and I'll see you tomorrow."

The light from the computer monitor went to black, leaving the Delivery Man sitting in the dark, enjoying the lights of the city from his high-rise condo…with his feet raised and a snifter of his favorite cognac in his hand.

CHAPTER 13

The Short Backstory Of Larry Becker

Larry Becker and Wendy Vaughn were having another loud, sweaty fuck-session in one of San Francisco's better hotels. Each was attractive and had a body designed for sex, with Larry being 38 and Wendy a decade younger.

After they collapsed in satisfaction, Wendy crawled to the night table on her side of the king-size bed. Once there, she picked up a small straw and a powder-covered mirror, carved four lines with a credit card, snorted two, then held them in his direction. As he did his hits, Wendy asked, "When, Larry? I'm tired of hotels."

With his back against the headboard and a head full of cocaine, Larry answered, "Don't rush it. What's today? October thirty-first, right? Only a couple of weeks to go. The lawyer's still fixing things with the judge. *Fuck* Community Property. There's ways around it, and if I do this right I'll get everything *she* worked for, and everything her family *gave* her." He carved two more lines, snorted them, then disturbingly grinned and imparted, "It'll all be mine."

When he put the paraphernalia on his night table, Wendy sternly said, "You mean *ours*."

He promptly replied with a smirk, "No, Wendy…I *don't*. But if you're a good girl, I'll let you come over and touch it once-in-a-while."

He may have thought her look of anger was an act, but Wendy knew it wasn't as she uttered, "*Bastard*," then rolled on top of him for their next marathon fuck-session.

Larry and Wendy were sitting on a bench outside the courtroom where he had spent the last two hours. As they kissed, his attorney, Phillip Cascone, walked out and approached the couple.

"So?" Larry stood up, wanting to know.

Cascone victoriously replied, "Like I told you months ago...half of the business was the *least* you'd get. But once she started going to that shrink, she was so whacked on medication she couldn't think straight. That's when her case fell apart. So as of today, November tenth, the company is *yours*. Of course..." He bent toward his client and whispered, "...there was that envelope to the judge."

Larry laughed, knowing it would turn out the way he and his lawyer planned.

That was when the distraught and catatonic 35 year old Diane was led from the courtroom by her attorney and several family members. Seeing Larry, Diane's father slowly approached him, dragging an oxygen tank behind his walker.

Staring at the man who turned his daughter into a walking vegetable, as physically and emotionally painful as it was, Diane's father yelled as best he could, "I don't know how you did this, you son-of-a-bitch, or how you stole everything we gave our daughter! But someday, you bastard...*someday* I'll get you! I swear I'll--"

Larry's attorney jumped in, "You may want to reconsider threatening my client, Mr. Johnson. Otherwise, I'll have you back in court before you know what hit you."

Family members rushed over and pulled the crying man away, causing Diane to break down and faint onto the granite floor.

Unconcerned about his unconscious ex-wife, Larry grabbed Wendy's hand and commanded, "C'mon, let's get the fuck outta here," then pulled her up and they strode from the scene.

Several feet away, leaning against the wall...the Delivery Man watched and listened to it all.

The couple drove to Boulevard, their favorite restaurant, to celebrate Larry's divorce and the acquisition of a successful business the Johnson family started two generations earlier and had given to Diane as a wedding present only four years ago.

As the sun began its slide into the Pacific, Larry and Wendy were in the president's office on the second floor of Johnson's Restaurant Supply Company. The lights were out, with only the last solar rays coming through the windows.

Around the room were two dozen photographs of Diane with Larry and her family.

Sprawled across one of the two desks was a naked and erotically loud Wendy fucking Larry.

Taking a break to snort more coke, Wendy pointed to a picture of Diane and asked, "Ever fuck *her* on your desk like that?"

Snorting his lines, he grinned sarcastically, "Oh yeah, and on *her* desk, too."

Raising her hand to slap him, he grabbed it, kissed and licked it…then laid Wendy atop Diane's desk where they fucked for another hour.

CHAPTER 14

Smile! You're On Candid Camera!

Chinese food containers mixed in with the case folders, photographs and notes around Valentine's office. Stacked neatly and in order of "victim-and-dates," there were thirty-four DVDs on the desk. The computer's clock showed 10:52PM.

Pai Lee and Agent Jordan were on the couch staring at the TV screen. With the remote in one hand and a food container in the other, she had a *very* big smile on her face.

Jordan looked at the Special Agent in awe. She found him. She found the Delivery Man.

The screen was paused on a black-&-white image of the killer's face.

Even though she was smiling, Valentine barked into the phone headset, "I don't care *what* time it is and I don't care *where* he is. You just find him and tell him I found the hitter." The Special Agent couldn't be prouder when she said it. She listened to the person put in charge of finding her boss at nearly 11 o'clock on a Monday night, then responded, "Yeah, we've been looking for a recurring face at the R.O. hearings and the divorce trials for *two weeks*…it was a fuckin' *bitch*, but we found him."

Agent Jordan was honored to be included in the "we found him" comment. He thought he had been invited nearly every night simply because he picked up and delivered the take-out food.

Valentine continued giving orders to the listener.

"I want this guy's smile run through the FR Scanner first thing in the morning, got it?" Again she listened, then gave her last command, "Yeah, just set it up. I don't want to hear any shit about it. We've watched eight trials in as many states…and the same face came up in each of 'em. This gets top priority, unless *you* wanna deal with Asac," then disconnected the call and pressed the remote's Play button to watch the courtroom video of the James and Valeria Lomax divorce hearing from four separate cameras and angles.

Valentine pointed to Valeria and told the young agent, "She's the one they found in Brooklyn propped up on the toilet in this fancy bathroom last February. Her boyfriend was sleeping in the bedroom when it happened sometime during the night. When he woke up and went to take a leak… voila! There she was. A bullet to the forehead, then eight more in random locations. The boyfriend heard nothing, so it was obviously a silencer. Right away the local police fingered the ex-husband for the murder until they found out he was picked up on a vagrancy charge the night before and he was sittin' in some jail getting' the shit kicked out of him and raped while his wife was popped around forty miles away. Somewhere there's justice in there about her getting whacked just for causing her husband's life to get so fucked up. Like most of the others I talked to, this guy had a great job before any R.O. or divorce paperwork…then it was all downhill after that."

She shared a moment of quiet contemplation with Jordan over what she just said, then continued, "By the time I got to James…he didn't have a clue as to who could have killed her." Valentine recalled questioning him and remarked, "Though there was one twinge of something when I mentioned she was found on the toilet."

Agent Jordan watched her…waiting for the finish.

"He smiled. The fact that she was murdered, *that* destroyed him. It brought him to tears whenever we spoke about it. But when I mentioned the toilet…he smiled. It had to have meant *something*, but he wouldn't say."

What Special Agent Valentine didn't know was that four months before Valeria had James removed from their home, she had seductively talked him into renovating their master bathroom to the tune of $42,000, and drove him crazy about finding, "…the most beautiful and perfect toilet for my beautiful and perfect ass."

That was why he smiled.

Valentine pointed to the screen and watched the hitter follow Valeria out the courtroom doors, then said, "Now I just have to find out who this guy is, where he's going next, and how he was in all these places, yet there's no record of the same name being in the same cities and towns for any of the hits."

Laughing more to herself than to the person she was speaking to, she continued, "You know, Jordan, I think it's gonna be a bigger sweater than I thought by the time this is over."

"More threads, ma'am?" the agent inquired.

Valentine smiled to herself and answered, "Yep, threads, peng you."

Seeing that her words confused him, she translated it.

"Peng you. It means 'my friend' in Mandarin."

He grinned and sat back as Pai Lee rewound the scene, then froze the screen on a clear shot of the Delivery Man's face. Staring at it with interest, she said to Agent Jordan, "Remember Monday, November fourteenth as the night we found the face of our killer."

The next morning, Valentine was in Barrett's office at 9:05AM. The same frozen image that was on her TV the night before was now on his. The computer monitor was noticeably missing…and the room was clean.

"This motherfucker sure got around over the last eleven months. I had the Tech Department edit all of his appearances onto one disk," Valentine said, proudly standing with the remote in her hand.

"When? You only found this face last night!"

"Around one-thirty this morning. What the fuck…they were there anyway. Might as well give them something to do. We had it all together by six. Is this great, or what?"

"Don't you ever sleep, Pai Lee?"

That was when the office door opened, causing Barrett to give a *big* smile. His new secretary entered with a cup of coffee and a file. She was in her late 50s and looked like she had as much time in the agency as the person she was now working for. Placing the coffee and file on his desk, she smiled then efficiently walked out.

"Happy now?" Valentine asked her boss.

Grinning, he looked at the TV screen and blissfully answered, "You pegged the hitter, and I've got a secretary. Yes…I'm happy."

After stopping by her husband's name etched into the hallway memorial, Valentine went directly to the door that read, "Facial Recognition Laboratory." Quickly stepping inside, she went right to the female technician assigned to the case and slid the DVD into the transport tray, then froze the first image of her prey.

"You've got thirty-one images of this guy on there. I wanna know who he is and I wanna be called the second you know. Roger that?"

The tech had already started the laser grid that enveloped and scanned the Delivery Man's face as she answered, "Loud and clear. As soon as we know, you'll know."

Valentine wasn't happy about having to wait, but she knew that once they came up with a name, a major thread in the 9 Millimeter Case would be revealed.

CHAPTER 15

Rixey

The same morning Valentine was in the Facial Recognition Laboratory, due to the 3 hour time difference, the Delivery Man was sitting in Gallagher's Steakhouse on 52nd Street in Manhattan with Richard Hartman, each ready to carve into his half of a Porterhouse for two.

Hartman was in his late 50s, had a professional air and appearance about him, regardless of what profession he might have been in. Like his dining partner, he was dressed in a finely tailored suit. It was apparent to anyone around them that these men were friends. Good friends.

Between chews and drinks of beer there was business that needed to be discussed. Hartman handed over a manila envelope and said, "Sorry to have you come to the city on such short notice, Rixey. It's time for another package to go to San Francisco, and I know how much you enjoy dealing with Little Billy. You've got to be there in a few days to meet The Major."

Whether he was enjoying the food or his new assignment, the Delivery Man, known to Hartman as 'Rixey,' smiled and cheerfully assured him, "Good. I was *hoping* to get back there."

Opening the large envelope, Rixey pulled out a smaller one inside containing a driver's license, two credit cards and an airline itinerary all made out to "Tim Voorhis," causing Rixey to chuckle, "Where the hell do you come up with these names?"

"Tim's the bass player in my kid's band," was the response, causing both men to laugh. That was when Hartman slid a small suitcase that was under the table from his side to Rixey's...then they enjoyed the rest of their lunch, conversation and friendship.

Valentine, once again in sweatpants and a T-shirt, now ferociously doing sit-ups on the office floor, was yelling into the phone headset,

"Whatdya *mean* you don't have a name? You've come up with faces in the past with fewer images! You got a clear shot of this guy's face from every-friggin-angle!"

Standing up and walking to the desk, she listened to the FR technician explain, "What can I tell you? We ran him through *our* files, all branches of the military, the CIA, DEA, ATF, Homeland Security, Interpol, Scotland Yard--"

The Special Agent didn't want to hear the list. She wanted a name.

"There's got to be *something!* Somewhere there's a picture and a file on this guy. *Find it!*"

"Yes, ma'am," sheepishly came the reply.

Pissed off, Valentine barked, "Then why are you wasting time talking to *me?* Go find this fuck!"

CLICK...the technician hung up. The pride and confidence Valentine had been feeling visibly left her. Even she saw it.

It was three days before Thanksgiving and the airports were already crowded, but once Rixey got to the Avis counter, he was grateful for getting away from the mania of holiday travel.

Being handed another set of keys and an offer to join their Preferred club, the rental agent finished off with a smile and, "Welcome to San Francisco, Mr. Voorhis, and thanks for choosing Avis!"

The Hyatt Hotel's bellman wheeled the luggage cart into a guestroom, placed two suitcases on stands, took his tip and departed. No sooner was he out the door before Rixey swiped a special key-card across the front of the larger suitcase causing it to unlock. He first removed a couple of suits and hung them in the closet. Once the suits were taken away, a shoulder holster, a metal box and two folders became visible.

Unlocking and opening the box, his pistol, a silencer, ten loaded 8-round magazines, a box of shells and gun-cleaning equipment were each neatly secured in perfect foam cut-outs. On top of the pistol was a pair of black leather gloves. One of the folders had "Embarcadero Enterprises" written on it. The other read, "Larry Becker."

Then he placed the smaller suitcase that Richard Hartman gave him on the bed. Swiping a key-card across the front, the locks popped open.

Looking inside, he showed no reaction at seeing it loaded with ten-million dollars in neatly stacked-and-wrapped $100 bills.

He closed the suitcase, locked it, then went to the door and secured all the locks before disrobing and stepping into the shower. He had a long night ahead of him.

Most of the businesses in the office building Rixey was visiting had locked their doors hours earlier. But having been there many times before, he knew where he had to go on the third floor and what to do once he got there.

Dressed in a suit and carrying the cash-filled suitcase, he approached the door that read, "Embarcadero Enterprises." He knocked twice, then looked directly into the security camera.

A buzzer sounded, allowing him entry.

In the reception area was the casually dressed male receptionist holding a .45 semi-automatic poised at the door as Rixey entered. None of this rattled him. He had done it before. Without any words being said, he approached the receptionist, slowly removed his Walther from its holster and placed it on the desk.

Both men nodded to each other, then with the .45 still pointed at him, Rixey walked to a door leading to an inner office and stared at another security camera. A grid of laser light scanned his face and another buzzer sounded, allowing the door to be opened.

Stepping inside, Rixey placed the suitcase on a conference table, opened it and looked across the room at The Major, a dedicated military man, 46 years old, dressed in an Army uniform...with his name equaling his rank.

Without hesitation, both men saluted one another, then The Major said, "Good to see you again, Rixey."

"It's good to see *you* again, Major...and I'm glad things are moving forward with the new regime."

Looking at the suitcase, The Major replied, "Thanks to *you* as usual, my friend." Realizing they had slipped from their military decorum, The Major got serious, gave another salute and said, "Dismissed."

The meeting of the two friends had ended as fast as it started.

Rixey returned the salute, did a slick military about-face and walked out the same door he came in.

Without saying a word to the receptionist, but with another nod, he picked up his weapon and, like Elvis, left the building.

CHAPTER 16

How Hot?

It was only a 20 minute drive from his meeting with The Major to the Market District and onto a street of warehouses and businesses just off the San Francisco-Oakland Bay Bridge. Once again, the Delivery Man stopped to admire the view as his phone's GPS brought him to the front of Johnson's Restaurant Supply Company.

Noticing the florescent light from the second floor office, he parked a block from the entrance and opened the "Larry Becker" folder to brush up on a few facts before taking it and getting out of the car.

Larry was sitting behind Diane's desk writing a check in the company checkbook. With it being close to Thanksgiving, the last couple of months have always been a banner period in the restaurant supply business...and Larry was enjoying it every way he could.

A four-grand pile of pocket cash sat next to a mirror, straw and pre-carved lines just waiting to get sucked up someone's nasal cavity. And as soon as he ripped the check out, that was exactly what he did.

Lifting his head from the second hit, Larry heard a metallic banging noise. Raising an eyebrow, he listened closer. The noise stopped. But now he was wired and paranoid. Nervously reaching down, he pulled a small .25 revolver from an ankle holster, then walked to the office door, turned on the hallway lights and yelled, "Hey! Who's down there? Wendy?" There was no response. Under his breath he muttered, "Fuck."

Filled with cocaine-courage and with the gun shaking in front of him, he descended the staircase that went to the showroom. Step-by-step he called out to whoever may have been there, "I got a gun, asshole! I don't want any trouble, so just get the fuck out. Don't do something stupid, 'cause I'll shoot you."

Entering the showroom, he flipped two switches, bathing everything in light as it reflected off large aluminum and stainless steel industrial restaurant equipment. Larry was sniffling and sweating as he apprehensively patrolled an aisle of stoves, cash registers, ovens, meat slicers and large coffee makers.

His eyes caught something as he approached one of the industrial dishwashers. The file bearing his name stood upright on it...so he stepped closer.

From behind, Larry Becker felt the barrel of the Delivery Man's silencer against his back.

"Hi Larry," were the words he heard that made him freeze. "Now put your hands up and give me that cute little cap-gun you got there."

As the recently divorced man raised his arms, the Delivery Man's black gloved hand took the revolver and slipped it into his jacket pocket.

Fearing for his life, Larry pleaded, "Look, man...I haven't seen your face. What the fuck you want? Money? There's money upstairs on the desk. There's blow, too. Take it all...just don't shoot."

Paying no attention to the ramblings of money and coke, the Delivery Man asked, "Why not? Why *shouldn't* I shoot you? What have *you* done that makes your life worth saving?"

There was silence. Larry had nothing to say.

The Delivery Man took two steps back and commanded, "Turn around."

Nervously quivering as he turned, Larry realized he wasn't facing a robber or a junkie, but a well-dressed man pointing a 9 millimeter Walther at his chest.

"Who *are* you? A cop?" Larry fretfully asked, then quickly followed it with, "I don't know *whose* coke that is! I found it in one of the vans. I'm gonna fire the driver tomorrow--"

The Delivery Man didn't want to hear anymore.

"Quiet. It's bad enough people like you exist. It doesn't mean I have to listen to you."

Letting the coke in his system do the talking, Larry continued, "What's with the file? Did Diane's father send you?"

"I said, '*Quiet!*'"

Looking at the gun, Larry realized he should do what he was told.

The Delivery Man scanned the showroom, slowly articulating as his stare returned to the company's new owner, "You want to talk? Then tell me what you know about restaurant equipment. This is a showroom... *show me* something."

Still shaking, and not choosing his words wisely, Larry responded with, "What are you? Fuckin' crazy?"

The pistol's barrel was raised from Larry's chest to his head as the Delivery Man smirked, "Amuse me," then nodded toward the 17-foot long industrial dishwasher. "Like *this* machine. What's it do?"

Larry moved his eyes for only a second to look at it and replied, "It's a dishwasher."

"That's a lot bigger than the one in *my* place," came the sarcastic response.

"It...it...it's for restaurants, hotels and stuff," stuttered the jumpy Larry.

"Expensive?"

Larry could only nod and sweat.

"How much, Larry?"

The new business owner had no idea and could only shrug.

Raising his voice, which caused it to echo off the concrete floor, walls and metal appliances, the Delivery Man bellowed, "I said, '*How much?*'"

Sorrowfully and nervously, Larry answered, "I...don't...know."

With a mixture of anger and playfulness, the Delivery Man inquired, "You mean, you own a company that sells this equipment, and you don't know how much this thing *is?*"

Larry cowardly nodded and mumbled, "We have...we have salesmen who do that."

"But according to that file, you *started working here* about six years ago as a salesman, didn't' you?"

The accused wept and lowered his eyes, knowing he was caught.

The Delivery Man shook his head in disappointment and continued to play.

"Well, wise guy, why don't you tell me what you *do* know about this model."

Larry tried to collect himself as the Delivery Man feigned interest.

"It...it cleans dishes. You put them in down that end." Larry pointed to the loading platform of the long machine. "Then they move through here on a conveyor belt," he continued pointing along the mid-section. "Then it stops in the middle and they're sprayed with real-hot water. Then they move into the dryer--"

Before Larry could say more, the Delivery Man interrupted.

"Real-hot water, huh?"

"Yeah," came another nervous response.

"*How* hot?"

Afraid and confused, Larry could only come up with a shrug and response of, "I don't know. *Real* hot."

Shaking his head in disgust, the Delivery Man angrily asked, "What *do* you know, Larry?"

A pool of urine formed at Larry's left foot.

"*I'll* tell you what you know, Larry. You know how to use the law to fuck people out of something that doesn't belong to you...and you have *no idea* how much I hate that. But I digress. You know how to snort coke and piss in your pants. You're a big man, aren't you, Larry?"

Realizing what this was all about, Larry stood...weeping. That was enough for the Delivery Man. He whacked Larry on the head with the butt of the Walther, knocking him unconscious and onto the floor.

A short time later the Delivery Man was standing at the dishwasher's loading platform. A still unconscious Larry, his hands, legs and feet now bound with heavy duty electric cords found "On Sale" in a display case, was face-up on the conveyor belt.

The machine had been turned on and steam was rising from the center.

"Larry? C'mon, buddy. Time to wake up," came from the Delivery Man as he lightly slapped the sleeping man's face.

Larry's eyed flickered open...unsure of where he was.

"Larry, I want you to answer this. What did Diane do that made you want to clean her out?"

Realizing he was on the conveyor and that his limbs were bound, he screamed, "It wasn't me! It was Phillip! Phillip Cascone! My lawyer! *He* told me how to get her out of the house! *He* told me how to do it! *He* made the deal with her shrink and the judge!" Tears exploded from Larry's eyes.

"But you went through with it, didn't you? You could've said 'No,' *right?*" the Delivery Man asked as he tapped the conveyor's Start button, causing the belt to slowly move.

"*Wait! Stop!*"

With the two men's eyes glued to each other, the Delivery Man put his index finger to his lips and whispered, "*Shhhhhh.*"

The conveyor inched the squirming-to-break-free Larry toward the dishwasher's entrance. Above the machine's noise the Delivery Man said, "Now let me teach *you* something you should already know. The water inside this particular model goes to two-hundred-and-twelve degrees. That's hot enough to kill germs, bacteria…and *you.*"

Just as Larry's head entered the tunnel, the Delivery Man joked, "And I bet it'll take that pee stain out of your pants, *too.*"

Once Larry's body was inside the dishwasher, he started to sweat and gasp for breath from the intense heat. That was when he started screaming, knowing what was coming next.

The conveyor automatically stopped and "real hot" water sprayed Larry from one-hundred small jets.

Larry deafeningly cried and screamed in pain while the Delivery Man walked to the center of the machine and spoke as loud as he could.

"Larry? Can you hear me? Listen close! The cleaning is from Diane. *This…*is from me."

A bullet ripped into the stainless steel and Larry's screams went silent. The Delivery Man chuckled at the water that poured from the hole.

Larry began screaming and wailing again…just not as loud.

Seven more bullets went into the machine, which caused the screaming to stop for good. Water flowed from the eight holes, but now it was mixed with blood.

The conveyor restarted as the Delivery Man picked up the file and watched Larry's bound, boiled, bloodied body emerge from the other end and fall from the belt onto the concrete floor.

Looking at his latest victim, the Delivery Man knew he had one bullet left…and put it in Larry Becker's forehead.

Then he turned off the showroom lights and left.

The Delivery Man drove to the Embarcadero and sat on the brick wall under the bridge enjoying the view. When he was sure no one was nearby, he nonchalantly dropped Larry's cap-gun into the water, then removed his leather gloves and went to Boulevard to eat.

It was his favorite place when he was in San Francisco.

CHAPTER 17

Life Comes Around And Gives You An Enema

Pai Lee Valentine's office was dark, lit only by the glow of the TV screen showing a paused image of the Delivery Man's face. She stared at it intensely as she sat alone on the couch eating her take-out Thanksgiving dinner...Peking Duck.

"C'mon, you good-lookin' son-of-a-bitch. Who are you? *Gimme* something. What happened to you that makes you want to track these people down and whack 'em?" Looking closer at the screen with a glint of interest and a tinge of infatuation, she pressed Play causing the video to continue. "You're smart I'll give you that. But how do you do it? How do you move across two continents with the same weapon?"

She watched the edited segments until she fell asleep on the couch... again.

The following morning, the streets of downtown Manhattan were deserted due to the holiday weekend with revelers recuperating from Macy's parade and their turkey's tryptophan.

A black Cadillac Escalade, with heavily-tinted bulletproof windows and New York plates, swiftly maneuvered to the underground garage of the Freedom Tower at One World Trade Center and passed through the security and military checkpoints before stopping in front of a special set of elevators guarded by four Marines in full-combat gear and armament.

Rixey stepped from the back door wearing a suit and an ID badge showing his picture and a bar-code. No name appeared on the badge. One of the sentries stepped in front of him as the others raised and poised their rifles. The solider pulled a laser gun from its holster and scanned the ID badge. A green light and beep emanated from atop the gun, then the two men saluted and Rixey was allowed to pass.

The door to an elevator opened...with another armed Marine positioned inside.

Rixey was taken to an unmarked floor, then an armed escort led him along a hallway to large double-doors with American flags on each side and two uniformed Marines standing at attention holding M-16's and wearing 9mm Berettas. The logo on the door read "National Security Agency" with its motto "Defending Our Nation. Securing The Future" beneath it.

Knowing what to do from there, Rixey saluted his escort, who sharply returned it, then made a perfect about-face and went back to his post. Rixey looked at the security camera. A laser grid scanned his face and sounded the required tone, causing the sentries to step aside as the doors swung open.

Walking along a corridor of windowless offices, Rixey turned into one bearing the nameplate, "Colonel Richard Hartman." After the standard salutations that would happen between old friends, the two men sat at Hartman's desk and got down to business.

"How was your trip, Rixey?"

"Fine," then he showed a more personal side and said, "I just don't like being unavailable for the few clients that I *do* have."

Hartman chuckled, "I don't get it. None of my other agents do anything but play golf and go to their kids or grandkids recitals, swim-meets and soccer matches. What's this need you're fulfilling by being a lawyer?"

Rixey humorously and teasingly shot back, "Not just a lawyer. A *divorce* lawyer."

"Fine. A *divorce* lawyer. Why?"

Not wanting to tread in that direction, Rixey responded with, "It's personal," then changed the subject. "Now, Colonel...what's so important that I had to come in?"

"It's The Major. The deal went bad," Hartman explained. "Little Billy agreed to our terms and accepted the package you delivered. But when he went back home...nada. Or I should say, khong tim duoc gi ca."

"It's not like they don't know who they're playing with," Rixey offhandedly responded, then realized something. "When did *you* start speaking Vietnamese?"

The Colonel answered, "The late eighties. I was in my early-thirties and stationed there for a couple of years." Returning to the topic-at-hand, he continued, "I haven't put you on an operation like this for quite some time, Rix...but The Major asked for you. He mentioned you were happy to see things progressing. Besides, it's part of your sector in the 'Asian community.' If the shit *did* hit the fan, you would be brought in anyway. But we want to avoid the fan getting hit. Do you understand?" He finished with a wink that was understood by the recipient.

What angered Rixey was the fact that what went down was done correctly by the American government, then accepted by the other side who had no intention of living up to an age-old agreement, so he spoke his mind a bit louder than his usual volume within those walls.

"We've been dealing with them for years...but *this? What is it* with these new guys? Doesn't *anyone* play by the rules anymore?" Taking a breath and a couple of seconds to calm down, he asked, "Where are these pricks now?"

Hartman knew he chose the right agent to deal with Little Billy. He answered, "Los Angeles. Surveillance is on them right now. In a few hours we'll know whenever he takes a shit. Be ready to move out in the next couple of days. The local authorities and military will give you anything you need on this. Your travel package will be ready after lunch."

"Yes sir." Thinking for a couple of seconds, he continued with, "I only have a couple of cases, and I'm sure I'll be back before they'll need me."

Having taken care of business, Hartman toyed with his friend, saying, "You know, if I really wanted...I could find out why you do it."

Rixey slapped both hands to his face in mock fear and yelled out, "*No! Not the sodium pentothal! Not that!*"

Both men shared a laugh at the response, then Rixey sat back, looked at his friend and said, "Here, this should keep you quiet for a while." Taking a deep breath, his face took on a serious aspect as he told Hartman, "It was something Caroline asked me to do. I couldn't tell her what I was *really* doing," giving the Colonel a knowing look. "So I went to law school."

Hartman quickly shot in, "After years of being a Marine and working for *us*."

"I was thirty-four. I had to do *something!* I had money, insurance, a house, a car...and no job. I *needed* a front."

Hartman sarcastically interjected, "So you got your degree, put out your shingle and started taking on cases."

Inquisitively, but with a slice of humor, Rixey asked, "Wow, you guys are good. How'd you find *that* out?" knowing Hartman and the agency weren't aware of *everything* he did.

"Maybe you didn't see the sign on the door when you walked in. We know *everything* about *everybody*," Hartman dryly replied.

The two men laughed again. Hartman then said something that changed Rixey's happy expression.

"And then…it happened."

Rixey's smile disappeared. Whatever "it" was, it pained him to be reminded.

Regretting he had caused his friend a stab of anguish, Hartman tried to make it better by finishing with, "It's always when you think everything's going your way that life comes around and gives you an enema." Then he shook his head and looked away.

Rixey could only nod in agreement.

After a moment of uncomfortable silence, Rixey broke it with, "Didn't somebody say something about lunch?"

"Is Gallagher's okay?"

"As long as it's not leftover turkey. I'm not a fan. Never was," Rixey threw in.

"I'll make a note of that in your file," Hartman jokingly replied, grateful Rixey didn't hold a grudge about him bringing up painful memories.

"Paula, show me Spousal Abuse Hearings in L.A. three and four days from now."

In the few seconds it took Paula to go to the proper sites and pages, the Delivery Man sat at his desk to eat his microwaved late-Thanksgiving dinner…Peking Duck.

After compiling the requested information, Paula began reading, "Los Angeles, California. Tinseltown. La-La-Land. Home of The Dodgers, The Hollywood Walk Of Fame, The Hollywood Farmer's Market, UCLA, USC, The Academy of Arts--"

"Not now," he said, putting a piece of duck in his mouth and sipping from a glass of his favorite white wine, Greco di Tufo.

"Yes sir," came the quick reply as a variety of screens flashed by before showing, "Los Angeles County Civil & Family Court." Then it gave a list of names under "Spousal Abuse Hearings."

Forty-five minutes later, the Delivery Man was on his second glass of wine, the remnants of the duck were off to the side…and Paula's voice continued.

"Documents then show the plaintiff, Jack Page, refused the defendant's offer of counseling. Divorce papers have been filed and served, with the R.O. hearing currently set for eleven o'clock, Tuesday, November twenty-eighth in the--"

Having grown tired of listening to legal documents that frustrated and angered him, he interrupted Paula.

"Save this one, too. Book me an early flight to LAX on Monday the twenty-seventh, then run a diagnostic and shut down."

"Should I rent you a car?"

"No thanks. My friend is picking me up."

"Which name and credit card should I use?"

"It's company business," he replied with a laugh. "Use the license and cards I scanned earlier."

And she did.

The Delivery Man rose, then collected his plate and wine glass. Making his way to the door, Paula softly said, "Have a good evening, sir, and I'll see you tomorrow," then the lights went out as the door closed behind him.

CHAPTER 18

Are There Any Good Places To Eat In Malibu?

Another black Escalade with tinted bulletproof windows, this time bearing California plates, drove to the front of 11000 Wilshire Blvd. The rear passenger doors opened and from each side stepped The Major and Rixey wearing suits and NSA ID badges. Both badges showed photos and bar codes, but no names.

Before shutting the door, Rixey stuck his head in the vehicle to tell the driver, "Thanks for dropping my bags at the hotel. Let them know I'll be there later this afternoon."

Once the Cadillac drove away, Rixey looked at the address and tall structure before him and asked, "Why here?"

"Any port in a storm, amigo. We needed a car and an empty office to run the operation out of, and the FBI had them. We're in a storm, and they have the port," The Major replied on their walk toward the entrance.

The office was sparse. A desk, a phone with three lines, two windows, a flat screen TV with a DVD player and a couple of uncomfortable chairs. The Major sat behind the desk and Rixey was opposite him.

It was time to be filled in on what happened, so the Major began his story.

"I met with him and reviewed the terms of the same agreement we've had with the last regime for decades, and he agreed. I turned over the briefcase you gave me last week to Hiep Ton (pronounced: Hip Tun) and he assured us--"

Rixey smiled and let out, "Hiep Ton. My old friend, *Little Billy*."

"Yep, and he told me to say 'Hello,' by the way." The two men sarcastically smiled over it, then, "Anyway, he assured us everything would run as smooth as it did when Lai Nguyen (pron: Ly Winn) was alive. But once he got the funds…" The Major shook his head in disgust. "…everything we've been paying them for went right down the tubes, or actually…out to the beach."

"And when you reached out to him?" Rixey asked.

The Major smirked, "He's not taking our calls."

The anger was apparent in Rixey's expression and words.

"What the fuck is *with* these new guys? The last of the Phuong Hoang (pron: Fung Whang) dies, and these young fucks go and fuck it up." Realizing he was showing his rage, he took it back a little and asked, "Okay, what do we know? Where is he? And what was that about 'the beach'?"

The Major answered, "Surveillance reported he was *over*-obvious in everything he did. It was as if he *wanted* us to see him do it. He went right to a Malibu real estate office and used the ten million as a down payment on a compound in Point Dume, a beach community in Malibu about twenty-five miles from here…then he and his entourage took up residence a couple of days later."

Rixey sarcastically grinned, "Hmmm…must be a nice place. Secluded?"

"It's on the end of the bluff. Great ocean view. Nearest home is about a hundred, maybe a hundred-and-fifty yards away."

"I think we need to pay Little Billy a visit," Rixey determined.

"Like the beach?"

"Who doesn't?"

As they shared a laugh, Rixey voiced his hope, "Lunch first?"

"Let's go afterward. Surveillance says our friend is home, and it's going to take about fifty to sixty minutes to get there. Maybe more."

"To go twenty-five miles?"

"And that's *without* traffic," The Major confessed.

"Friggin' L.A. roads."

"Exactly," The Major agreed with another laugh.

"Then let's leave right now. The sooner we talk to Billy, the sooner we can eat."

"Stop reading my mind. That's an order!" the officer instructed.

Laughing, they rose and left the room.

Agent Jordan walked into Valentine's office and laid a folder on her desk. She opened it and scanned photos of Larry Becker's wet, bound, boiled, bloodied body lying on a concrete floor at the end of an industrial dishwasher.

Having become jaded since receiving the 9 Millimeter Case, Valentine laughed at a photo that, at one time, would have disgusted and angered her, and said, "*Shit!* This guy must have been a *real* prick." Realizing she shouldn't have uttered that in front of her subordinate, the Special Agent shook herself back to reality.

Jordan was wise enough to change the subject.

"If we didn't have those videos, I'd think he was invisible. Any idea how you're going to find him?"

"Not yet. But I'm on it." Placing the photo on the desk, she asked, "You hungry? I need lunch."

Always happy to be in her company, Jordan would have said "Yes!" if he had just come from eating a tuna salad sandwich. Valentine grabbed a recently put-together file of her prey's photographs extracted from the videos, and they headed out the door.

Waiting at the elevator bay, Valentine and Agent Jordan perused the photos. When the doors opened, they secured the file, entered, turned and faced the closing doors…oblivious to the other four occupants.

Two of them were Rixey and The Major.

Still in their humorous mood, Rixey leaned to his associate and jokingly asked, "Are there any good places to eat in Malibu?"

Overhearing the question, the two FBI agents looked at one another with an "Is this guy serious?" glance.

Joking back, The Major snickered, "Yeah, a few."

Everyone except Rixey and The Major stepped into the lobby when the doors opened. Those on their way to visit Little Billy continued to the underground garage for a "company car."

As Valentine and Jordan walked from the elevator bay, she made sure no one was behind them, then shook her head and jokingly said, "Friggin' out-of-towners."

Walking to Veterans Avenue and finding their usual table in a local eatery, Agent Jordan skimmed through the file as Valentine appeared to be reading a menu that she knew by heart. But her mind was *really* on the man in the photos and videos.

"How's that sweater coming along, ma'am?"

Bringing her back to reality, she stuttered, "Huh?"

"Your threads. Do you have enough to determine why this guy went after the specific people he chose?"

"You mean *besides* the fact they were scumbags? I've been thinking…I need to see what goes on at a Spousal Abuse Hearing. It may give me a better idea." Raising an eyebrow, she followed it with, "I'm not gonna be in the office tomorrow."

The waiter brought their tuna salad sandwiches and Valentine went back to her thoughts.

CHAPTER 19

I Will Not Fail You

Once the black Buick Enclave Avenir SUV passed the traffic jam caused by the malfunctioning light at Malibu Canyon Road, it was finally able to cruise north on the Pacific Coast Highway. The Major drove while he and Rixey enjoyed the view of the ocean to the left and the Santa Monica Mountains on the right. Along the way, they called Surveillance to make sure Elvis hadn't left the building.

He hadn't.

Having a thought, Rixey asked, "What's the plan? We gonna knock on the door and tell him we want our money back?"

The Major kept his response official with, "The objective is to get things back to the way they were…and to let Billy and his tough guys know who's in charge. Right now, he thinks it's him. Besides, this isn't the kind of neighborhood where you knock on a door."

Rixey assuredly articulated, "Don't worry. We'll let them know who's in charge soon enough."

With that, the SUV turned left at the sign that read "Point Dume."

"Interesting name," Rixey said in passing. He didn't know he had stumbled onto one of The Major's quirks of L.A. trivia knowledge.

"In the seventeen-hundreds it was named after Francisco Dumetz from the Mission of San Buenaventura. When the map of the coast was made, obviously by someone unfamiliar with Spanish surnames, it was misspelled to Dume. Such is the lack of knowledge and fact-checkers throughout history. Oh, and Point Dume is where they shot the final scene in the original Planet Of The Apes where you see the top of the Statue Of Liberty."

Throughout The Major's tutorial, Rixey had been staring at him… quietly entertained by what he had just learned, more about his friend than about the name of the community they were driving through.

"Think we should pick up some pastry? I'd hate to show up empty handed," Rixey said with a serious face.

Again, the two men couldn't hold their laughter for more than a few seconds before letting it out.

Little Billy's opulent, two-level mansion was surrounded by a high wall on three sides and sat atop the Point Dume bluff. The rear of the property was massive, complete with a spectacular vista of the Pacific Ocean. The backyard's manicured lawn extended to the cliff where it dropped one-hundred-and-forty feet straight down to the beach. And everywhere within the walls of the property, armed men patrolled.

The Buick glided along the long circular driveway to the guard house attended by three suited, muscular Vietnamese men. One of them promptly approached, so The Major lowered his window.

At the same time, Rixey lowered his window to peer at the front wall's two security cameras that were trained on their vehicle. He smiled and waved at them.

Before the guard could utter a word, The Major showed his NSA ID and commanded, "Open up. We're here to see Hiep Ton."

The guard, speaking broken-English, inquired suspiciously, "He expect you? You have appointment? You have warrant?"

"We're old friends and just happen to be in the neighborhood," The Major replied in the most antagonistic way, and hoping Rixey wouldn't laugh.

"Who you?" the guard growled at the driver.

With that, Rixey opened his door, got out and raised his hands for everyone to see. The other two guards stepped outside holding 9mm Uzi's.

Loud enough for them to hear, and with all the confidence in the world, the American bellowed, "Tell him Rixey's here. That's all you need to know."

With the machine guns pointed at Rixey, the guard sneered, then walked to the guard house and picked up a phone. The visitors watched him speak to someone, hang up and return in short order.

Striding to the SUV arrogantly full of himself, the guard waved Rixey away and said, "He said he not home today. He call you when he want you come back."

Pissed off and showing it in his stance, Rixey lowered his voice and sarcastically responded, "Oh really? Is that what the little asshole said?"

Out of nowhere two more suit-wearing, muscular Vietnamese guards with Uzi's appeared next to the others.

Observing the situation and the hardware, the two Anglos took the high ground.

The Major got the attention of the guard and said, "Tell Little Billy we'll be back tomorrow."

"He said he call *you*, Yankee Man. And his name now *Mr.* Billy. No more *Little* Billy. That all *you* need to know," the guard said, ending it with a laugh.

Rixey stared at him for a few seconds, then just before getting in the SUV and closing the door, he said, "Di choi vui nhe…*ca chon*," for all to hear.

The guard's look of indignation was immediate. Those behind him grumbled and stepped forward with the four Uzi barrels pointed at the SUV.

Rixey raised his hand, waved and smiled as The Major put the vehicle in gear, drove around the driveway and out to the road.

"What did you say to Smiley, Rix?"

Rixey nonchalantly replied, "Have a nice day…*asshole*."

With the most serious of faces and slamming his hand on the steering wheel, The Major yelled, "*Jesus*, Rixey! Are you trying to cause an international incident?" as he maneuvered the local roads.

Only a few seconds of silence passed before both men could no longer contain their laughter…again.

Once they got to the Pacific Coast Highway and headed south, The Major asked, "What time are we coming back tomorrow?"

Rixey thought for a few seconds, then answered, "I don't know yet. There's something I have to take care of around ten. I should be at the office by noon. I'll meet you outside and we can go from there." Then he changed the subject to, "We're going to eat now, right?"

As the SUV reached cruising speed, The Major didn't notice the black Mercedes with the darkest of tinted windows following at a distance.

"Geoffrey's," The Major answered.

"What's Geoffrey's?"

The SUV turned right off the PCH, drove down the steep driveway into Geoffrey's parking lot where they were immediately attended to by a valet. Within a minute, the men walked to the host's desk, then were led to a table along the railing overlooking the ocean.

The black Mercedes slowly made its way down the driveway and into the lot. Lowering the driver's window, Little Billy's bodyguard, known only as *Big Man*, held a cell-phone and was looking at the approaching valet. With a vile stare and carnivorous growl, he said, "Go away, puny dog. Do not come near this car." Then the window rose…and the valet backed away.

Speaking into the phone, the conversation was in Vietnamese.

"I have them at Geoffrey's."

His boss's voice replied, "Don't kill them there. I like Geoffrey's. Stay with them. Call in whoever you need. Do not fail me."

Big Man's look turned vicious and determined as he watched The Major and Rixey be seated.

"On the bones and ashes of our forefathers, and the honor of our homeland…I will not fail you."

CHAPTER 20

All Rise!

It was 8:53AM when Special Agent Pai Lee Valentine stood before two courthouse guards presenting her Glock, an extra ammo magazine and FBI ID. Quickly passing through the Security Checkpoint, she found her way to the courtrooms holding Domestic Abuse and Spousal Abuse hearings.

Once again, it was a courtroom filled with unhappy people who were there for equally unhappy reasons. The only people smiling were the attorneys. Regardless of which side they represented, their billable hours started accumulating from the time they left home.

Just as Valentine made her way to a front row seat on the center aisle, the clock on the wall ticked to 9 o'clock. She didn't have time to sit before "All rise!" loudly came from the Court Clerk. And that's what everyone did.

From her jacket pocket, the FBI agent pulled at a picture of her target, then instinctively scanned the room…eyeing two cameras in the process.

The judge made his way to the bench, then let out a, "Be seated," followed by the clerk's ritual of informing everyone of where they were, the date and the introduction of "the Honorable-whoever-would-be-deciding-their-fate."

Valentine watched the proceedings intensely. So-much-so, she didn't notice the clock until 10:49. Some of the faces in the gallery had changed as the hearing in front of her continued.

The early-50's plaintiff, a facially-bruised woman, was on the stand answering her attorney's questions.

"My husband, he came home…drunk. He was mad. I don't know why. He wouldn't tell me. He came into the bedroom and woke me up."

"And then?" the attorney pressed.

"Then...he told me to get up and make something to eat. I told him to come to bed because he had to get up for work in a few hours." Tears of anguish and pain rushed from her eyes. "That was when he started hitting me."

Everyone in the courtroom focused on her still-bruised-and-swollen face from two weeks earlier.

The plaintiff continued, "He pulled off the covers. That was when he ripped my pajama bottom." With each word she found it harder to speak, until it only came out as stutters, "He...ripped off my...pajamas. He tried to--"

"I object!" the defense attorney stood and yelled.

After nearly two hours and three different horror stories all based on two people who loved one another at some point in their past, Valentine needed some air. Quietly, she walked up the aisle toward the big doors in the rear of the gallery.

Just as she pushed open one door to exit, a man entering the other accidently brushed against her. He turned and quietly said, "Excuse me. Sorry," then stopped to look...taken by her face.

She offhandedly responded, "No problem," not thinking twice and barely glancing in his direction, then each continued on their way.

As Valentine stepped into the marble hallway she stopped short, pulled out the photo of the face she now knew in her sleep...and stared at it.

Shocked to the point of not believing she walked right past him, she blurted out, "*Bu ke neng!*" meaning "*No way!*" in Mandarin.

Making a lightning-speed U-turn, Valentine rushed to the big doors, grabbed a handle and soundlessly re-entered the courtroom she couldn't wait to get out of less than two minutes earlier. Standing along the back wall, she watched the Delivery Man take a seat in the third row on the center aisle.

With the angriest of snarls on his face, the judge looked at the male defendant and barked, "Let it be shown and recorded as of today, November twenty-eighth, based on the defendant's record and the evidence put forth, I find in favor of the plaintiff. The Restraining Order will stay in place." Then he eyed the accused and continued, "If I find out you contact, talk to, or ever touch this woman again, I'll make sure you won't see daylight for a decade," then he banged the gavel and yelled, "Bailiff! Secure the defendant and return him to jail to finish his thirty day assault charge."

With a simple nod of the head, the bailiff put the husband's hands behind his back, cuffed him and led him away. His battered and crying wife was comforted by her attorney and a family member.

The Delivery Man was completely unaware Valentine's eyes never left him. The amazed look was still on her face. Not knowing if it was good luck or expert detective work, at that moment...she didn't care.

After a few minutes the judge signaled the clerk that he was ready for the next case.

"The court calls," the clerk looked at the names on a roster, "Page versus Page. All parties for Page versus Page!"

Visibly depressed and sullen, Shannon Page, a black 49 year old woman and her black female attorney rose from the audience and walked to the defendant's table. Jack Page, smiling, black, 56, and his well-dressed white attorney approached the plaintiff's table. No one saw the attorney give a quick wink to the judge.

That was all that needed to be done.

Valentine watched the Delivery Man lean forward in his seat, wanting to see and hear *everything*. She had no idea this was the case he came for.

It wasn't long before Shannon was on the stand, confused, near tears... and face-to-face with the prosecutor.

"I have *no idea* what he's talking about. I *never* touched him! I *never* did the things he's saying I did." She looked at the judge and wailed, "I never hit or threatened my husband *ever*, your honor. I *swear!* Me? With a knife?"

The grinning attorney asked, "Then why, Mrs. Page...why would he accuse you of doing so?"

It was the question that made her tears flow.

"I...don't...know," she struggled to get out. "That morning...when I was making breakfast...he told me he loved me. By that night he said he wanted a divorce."

The attorney smiled, looked at the judge and said, "No further questions."

An hour later, a sobbing Shannon stepped into the hallway being held and comforted by her attorney who led her to a bench along the wall. She needed to sit. No more than a minute later, Jack's attorney walked out... followed by his smiling client. He was followed by the Delivery Man... who was followed at a distance by the FBI agent.

The Delivery Man leaned against the wall and watched Jack shake his attorney's hand, then enter an elevator.

Valentine, twenty feet behind and against the same wall...watched him and everything he observed.

A taxi rolled away from the courthouse and through the streets of downtown L.A. on its way to the west-side and the entrance of 11000 Wilshire Blvd. Rixey sat back and was on his cell-phone. Behind his cab rolled another with Valentine in the backseat...watching.

"According to the driver, I should be there in about thirty minutes," he said. "Meet me at the entrance and we'll go see Billy from there."

The Major replied, "Surveillance says he hasn't left the house yet," then continued with a laugh, "Maybe you were right. Maybe we *should've* brought something. Want me to pick up some pastry? A cake?"

"Whatever makes you happy. I'll see you in a bit," and they ended the call.

It was about 1:40PM and just another day at the L.A. FBI Headquarters. People walked in and out of the front doors on their way to whatever they needed to do and wherever they needed to go. Rixey's cab pulled to the curb and let him out on the passenger side. He looked for the Buick Enclave SUV, but it wasn't there yet.

Seconds later the cab containing Valentine pulled up to the building where she had been hunting for the man now standing in front of its entrance. After paying the driver, she got out and stayed away from of his field of vision, wanting to make sure he didn't recognize her from their chance meeting in the courtroom's doorway. She mixed in with those passing by and stood against the building's white wall, keeping her head down just enough to see him.

It was only a couple of minutes before the Buick slowed and stopped in front of the building, as Valentine, though unable to hear, watched all.

The passenger window slid down to show The Major in the driver's seat eating a cannoli with a smile.

His partner and friend approached, stood on the curb, leaned into the open window and asked with a laugh, "Is that lunch? I was hoping we'd go back to Geoffrey's."

Holding up an open pastry box, The Major answered, "I couldn't help it, Rix…I was hungry. Think Little Billy will mind?"

Rixey, still laughing, said, "Listen, we have to stop at the hotel to pick up my gun. I don't wanna make this house-call without it."

The Major replied, "Roger that," as Big Man's Mercedes turned right off Sepulveda Blvd onto Wilshire, closely followed by a Hertz van.

"You want to drive?" the Major asked as he took another bite of the cannoli. "My wife had to take the kids to school for some '*parent thing*,' so I got *nada* for breakfast and these things were calling my name."

Again the two friends laughed and Rixey replied, "Sure."

Neither of them noticed the Mercedes and van slowing as they neared, and the van's side door opening.

The machine gun fire of two Uzi's erupted from the van, blasting the SUV and everything around it. Hearing the first burst, Valentine instinctively dropped to the ground and pulled her .40 from its holster under her jacket, unsure of what was happening.

Several bystanders were hit with stray and ricocheting rounds. People were screaming and running in all directions, making it harder for Valentine to see who was doing the shooting, though she was able to see Rixey kneel on the passenger-side of the SUV as it took multiple rounds on the driver's side.

Big Man's Mercedes still crawled while he watched from the driver's seat. Suddenly, with people screaming and the wounded calling out in pain, the shooting stopped. Two Vietnamese assassins stepped from the van and walked to the front of the SUV as they loaded new magazines into their Uzi's to finish the job they were sent to complete.

To kill Rixey.

Valentine stood with her .40, aimed and emptied it into them before they could get a round off. They dropped to the curb, causing tires to screech as the Mercedes and van sped away, sideswiping several cars and killing a motorcyclist.

With expert precision, Valentine popped out the empty magazine, slammed in a full one, aimed at her target and yelled, "*Freeze!*"

Amidst the chaos and carnage, Rixey rose with his head spinning between the disappearing vehicles and the armed FBI agent. He didn't hear her or the cries of the wounded. His eyes were on something else. Something horrific.

"I said, '*Freeze!*'"

Raising his hands to show he was unarmed, he looked at The Major, still wearing his seatbelt and with the cannoli in his right hand…dead. His upper body was riddled with bullet-holes. Rixey couldn't speak. He couldn't move.

Police and ambulance sirens wailed in the distance, and got louder and closer by the second. Several dead and wounded bodies littered the sidewalk. Traffic in every direction stood still.

Rixey, hands still raised and through watering eyes, turned toward Special Agent Valentine. For a second he thought he recognized her, then slowly turned to his dead comrade and friend.

Armed FBI agents from within the building and policemen converged on the scene. Valentine quickly pulled her FBI ID from her pocket and held it up while still pointing her weapon at Rixey.

Seeing the two dead Vietnamese hitters and their Uzi's, two policemen pointed their pistols at Rixey…as the shock of what happened to his friend slowly sank in.

CHAPTER 21

It Will Be Duly Noted In My Report

Chief Lombardi of the Los Angeles Police Department sat at his desk about 30 minutes after the Wilshire Blvd massacre. The media was already all over it. Three news helicopters and a police chopper nearly crashed over the San Diego Freeway. The latest body count in front of the FBI building was up to nine, counting The Major, the motorcyclist and two Vietnamese assassins. Two bystanders were on the Critical List, and six others were being treated for various levels of bullet wounds.

Sitting across from the chief was a very pissed off Special Agent Valentine. They were listening to the voice of Colonel Richard Hartman coming through the phone's speaker.

"...so it was fortuitous you were at the scene, Agent Valentine. I understand you--"

"*Special* Agent Valentine," she angrily interjected.

"Special Agent Valentine. I understand you were able to shoot two of them. Do we know their status, Chief Lombardi?"

"Both Vietnamese. Both dead, sir," came the reply.

"And I can be assured Rixey will be released and given every courtesy and assistance in this matter, correct?" Hartman checked.

Valentine was boiling in her own anger as the chief answered, "Whatever he needs, Colonel Hartman."

That was it...she had hit her pressure point.

"Wait a minute! There are some things *I* need to know about this guy!" she barked at the man in front of her and to the one on the phone. Chief Lombardi was stunned at her reaction.

Hartman calmly came back with, "I thought I made it clear, he's involved in a matter of national security. I thought you would've realized that after what happened in front of your office. Now, if I need to contact your superior, I'll be happy to, but I don't think you'll want that. Not unless you want to be filing reports for a few years." Then, to let her know he meant business, he finished it with, "I believe that would be Assistant Special Agent in Charge Fred Barrett, correct?"

Hearing her boss's name took a little wind out of Valentine as she replied, "Yes…sir," though she couldn't end it there. "But, I've been assigned to an investigation that--"

Hartman didn't want to hear it, cutting off whatever she had to say with, "Also let me remind you…the classified level of this operation means you communicate with *no one* about this event *or* this phone call. That order comes from the highest level. Am I clear?"

Chief Lombardi looked at Valentine and put his index finger to his lips, hoping she'd take the hint and keep her mouth closed.

Being told to be quiet angered her, along with having to take Hartman's orders, so her words came out slow…and low.

"Yes…sir.

Hearing what he needed to hear, the Colonel ended the call saying, "I want to thank you for your assistance and cooperation, Valentine. It will be duly noted in my report." Then the line went dead.

"That's *Special Agent* Valentine, *asshole!*" she barked at the speaker.

Frustrated, pissed off and wanting answers, she looked at Chief Lombardi. With determination in a voice that wasn't going to take "No" for an answer, Valentine growled, "I want him before he disappears."

"Why?"

Her reply was fast. "It has to do with an FBI investigation."

"And it will be off the record so I know nothing about it?"

Quickly turning it into a joke, she asked, "Nothin' about *what?*" and finished with a wink.

Before he could give *any* kind of retort, she was out the door.

It was a long ride in the bulletproof cruiser from Police Headquarters to The Beverly Hills Hotel. It was even longer because no one spoke the entire way.

Secured between Special Agent Valentine and the Kevlar-protected and helmeted driver was an M-16 attached to the heavily modified electronic dashboard. Seated comfortably in the back, Rixey read and sent texts on a secured federal application within his phone. Valentine looked ahead... with questions running through her mind at speeds even *she* couldn't keep up with.

All eyes were on the police vehicle as it made its way up the elegant and famous hotel's curved driveway. Once the cruiser came to a halt, three valets swiftly attended to each occupant's door. The driver let them know he was, "Just dropping off."

Valentine and Rixey exited the passenger doors and took a couple of steps before he looked at her and asked, "Where are *you* going?"

"We need to talk."

"Get back in the car. I don't have time," He headed toward the lobby and told her, "I have to see someone about what happened."

"I'll go with you," she declared without thinking, and as her ride pulled away. She increased her pace to keep up with him.

He was on a mission.

So was she.

He chuckled, "I don't think so."

Catching up to him, she looked straight ahead and chuckled back, "You don't have an option." Walking into the lobby, its opulence caught Valentine off-guard, causing her to quietly state, "The NSA has *this kind* of money? Nice."

Entering the elevator near the The Polo Lounge, he barely looked at her as he spoke.

"I need to get something in my room. You have me until then."

As the elevator made its way to the fourth floor and realizing she had a limited amount of time to find out everything she wanted to know, the FBI agent started her questioning.

"Why is the NS--"

He silently glared at her, put his index finger to his lips and pointed to the ceiling, letting her know there might be security cameras and microphones.

Though very pissed off, she edited herself with, "That's twice today I was told to be fuckin' quiet. I'm gonna want some answers."

Once they reached room 417, Valentine's mind was overloaded with what she wanted to know.

Rixey unlocked the door and headed directly to the closet. Valentine walked inside and leaned against the dresser. He reappeared wearing an empty holster and carrying the metal box.

She began her questioning with, "What's your name?

"Rixey," he responded as he threw the box on the bed, swiped the key-card and popped it open.

"Yeah, that's what Hartman called you," Valentine replied, impressed with the key-card, and while she watched him put four loaded magazines in slots on the holster's strap. "Is that a first name or last?" Then she got cocky and asked, "Or is it a code name? Like Condor?"

He stopped what he was doing for the time it took to answer, "Rixey. That's all you need to know," then smiled and returned to the box.

He didn't notice his new friend eyeing the silencer in its cut-out slot. Then she watched as he raised the 9mm Walther P38, popped in a magazine, loaded a round into the chamber, removed the magazine and replaced the first bullet…which made it nine. The he returned the magazine into the grip and holstered the weapon.

Valentine's eyes went *wide*. She raised her voice, exclaiming, "*No!* Now *I* need to know *more*. A *lot* more."

Again, Rixey stopped what he was doing, grinned and asked, "Yeah? Like what?"

As he turned to put on a sport jacket, Valentine replied, "Like what you know about Sherry Hoffman."

He was stunned, but didn't show it…though it stopped him from slipping on his jacket.

Seeing that she had his attention, Valentine continued, "Ronald Gladue? Duane Griffin? Theodore Schor? Gary Pogue? Pamela Adams? Larry Becker? Now *Larry? That one* was a *classic*. And a few others in America and Asia," then she pointed to his pistol and finished with, "All hit with that nine you've got there."

Calculating his response, Rixey turned to find he was facing her .40. He froze, not wanting to give her any reasons to pull the trigger.

"Who *are* you?" he asked.

"I'm not the Dread Pirate Roberts, *that's* for sure," she comically replied.

It took Rixey a few seconds to get the connection. Smiling at her wit, he said, "Good answer."

"Special Agent Pai Lee Valentine. FBI Serial Homicide Division…and I've been lookin' for you. And that's all *you* need to know. Now, you gonna talk to me?"

Having a reason to be concerned, Rixey asked, "Did you mention any of those names to the police or Colonel Hartman?"

"No."

"Why not?" he queried.

"That's *my* business. Right now, I wanna know why the National Security Agency is popping pricks who wrongfully accuse their spouses of Spousal or Domestic Abuse."

He calmed a bit in his stance and continued smiling…but now it was due to him being impressed.

"You figured that out?"

"Yes. And I wanna know why you were in that courtroom today?"

With the gun still trained on him, he expressed his happiness as he said, "That *was* you! I *knew* I recognized you. How'd you know I was going to be there? How'd you know who I was?"

"Easy, pal. *I'm* the one with the questions!" Keeping his hands visible and moving slowly, he sat on the bed as she kept going, "That you'd be there today? Dumb luck. No two ways about it. And how did I know it was *you?* I carry your picture in my pocket."

"*My* picture? Where'd you get *that?*"

"Courthouse security cameras."

Rixey made a "Yep, *that'll* do it" face and praised her with, "Now *that* was good detective work. *Excellent* job." Loosening up a little, he said, "Okay, all I'll tell you is this…the NSA had nothing to do with those hits."

Once again, Valentine's mind went into overdrive, asking, "Were you contracted by the ex-spouses or someone *close* to the ex-spouses?"

"Look…I'm gonna put my jacket on, so careful with that cannon." Then he laughed, "And *me? Contracted?* By *those* people? No. Not at all." Getting serious, he continued, "The only people who *pay me* to kill bad guys is our government."

Slipping on his jacket and before her next question, he asked, "You have a car?"

She made the same face she made to Agent Jordan in the elevator when she heard some guy ask if there were any good restaurants in Malibu, and responded with, "It's L.A., amigo. Of *course* I have a car. But it's at the office."

"We'll take a cab and get it. You know a place called Point Dume? I want to get there as soon as possible."

"Yeah. *Everyone* knows Point Dume. Why?" she asked, lowering the gun...a little.

"You know *why* it's called Point Dume?" he probed.

Unsure how that fit in, she shook her head and responded, "No."

"*I* do. You know how to speak Vietnamese?"

This time, without missing a beat she answered, "Chinese. Three dialects. No Vietnamese."

Closing, locking and returning the metal box to the closet, he said, "Bummer. C'mon, put that thing away and let's go."

That wasn't how she was going to work it. Raising the gun, she angrily contested, "*No!* I've been busting my ass too hard to get to this point. I want answers, and I want them *now!*"

"You want answers? Fine. We can talk on the way. The sun's gonna be down soon, and there's a lot to do. Now let's go!"

Valentine's dark blue 2015 Lexus GS350h cruised north on the Pacific Coast Highway with the last rays of the sun reflecting off the water just before disappearing. Since they left the FBI's Wilshire Blvd parking lot and while driving, Pai Lee hadn't stopped asking questions, but not before Rixey made her assure him there were no recording devices going.

"So you're saying that since the mid-seventies we've been giving the Phuong Hoang (pron: Fung Whang) ten million dollars a year to keep their gangs off American streets and under control? What's Phuong Hoang mean?"

Rixey looked over her Glock as he replied, "Soaring Eagle. And yeah, that's *exactly* what we've been doing. Think about it...for decades we've been trying to keep a lid on Japanese, Chinese and South Korean gangs, right? And that's not counting ones from Central and South America, and Russia. It took our government forty-something years just to get rid of the Mafia. With *all* of them, we started too late...and the big ones are now into things we can't stop, so it's costing hundreds-of-millions every year. My section, my '*community*,' contains certain parts of Asia regarding specific issues. Matters like *this* are one of them. You see, gangs from other countries are into violent wars among themselves, prostitution, slavery, drugs, the whole enchilada. After the Vietnam War, with the influx--"

"Conflict," the FBI agent interjected.

"Whatever." Popping out the .40's magazine and checking the type of bullets she used, he continued, "With the influx of refugees, we had to do something from the get-go to make sure they didn't do anything that would cost us billions to deal with down the road."

"So we give them money?" she questioned while shaking her head in disbelief.

Slapping the magazine into the grip, he replied, "Ten-fucking-million a year. That's kid-shit compared to what it would cost to deal with it on the streets and in the courts. That was the deal from the beginning and the old leaders always honored it. They used it to keep their street bosses from getting greedy." He stopped admiring her weapon and hoped to drive his point home. "Look, it costs us seventy-million-plus a year to deal with the Chinese gangs just in New York and San Francisco. And you *know* it's impossible to stay on top of them and every *other* group that's out there."

"I gotta agree with you on that," she said as she nodded her head.

"Think about this...when was the last time you heard about a Vietnamese drug war? Or a political kidnapping?"

"Can't say I have," she attested, then asked, "Okay, so what happened? What's that have to do with what happened today?"

"Little Billy." It pissed Rixey off just saying the name. "Once the last of the old bosses died, the toughest young one stepped up."

In Pai Lee's typically-cocky-fashion and while facing forward, she acerbically said, "And it looks like Little Billy has his own ideas on how things should be run. So he took the cash...then told the NSA and America to go fuck themselves," ending it with a sarcastic glance before returning her eyes to the road.

He looked at an incoming text on his phone, but stayed on the subject, "Yeah, except for one problem."

Valentine ventured a guess.

"The guy in the car you were talking to?"

An anger-tinged grin appeared on Rixey's face as the words, "And now it's payback time," left his mouth.

He handed her the pistol. While holstering it, she asked, "Are we going into this alone? Or are you calling in the cavalry?"

"The cavalry? We *are* the cavalry!" he laughed before returning to the phone's text, then asked while reading, "You know how to get to the Navy base at Point Mugu?"

She took her eyes from the road and looked at him as he typed into the phone, and said, "Of course." She was intrigued, oddly impressed and strangely enamored. He was the 9 Millimeter Killer she had been tracking for nine weeks, right down to the very day. He even *acknowledged* the killings. What was she doing even *thinking* of something amorous? It was her job to bring him to justice. Yet there she was, a Special Agent for the FBI going on a revenge mission in the name of the NSA and America.

She returned her eyes to the road as he continued texting. It was dark and Point Mugu was 22 miles away.

"Okay…next question," she pressed.

"Go."

"If the NSA wasn't behind the murder of all those people, you know I'm supposed to arrest you, right?"

He put the phone in his lap, thought for a few seconds, then looked at her to give the only answer he could come up with.

"Can we talk about that later over dinner? First, I gotta get some bad guys. Okay?"

She again took her eyes from the road and gave the only answer *she* could come up with.

"Seems you do that quite a bit."

Looking into her eyes, he said, "There's a lot of 'em out there."

Returning her eyes to the road, she pressed on the accelerator and sadly replied, "Yes there are."

CHAPTER 22

Operation Payback Concluded, Sir

Several armed guards walked the perimeter of Little Billy's walled Point Dume fortress. Their boss was certain the L.A. police and federal authorities would be showing up to discuss what happened earlier that day. Little Billy was so sure they'd be coming, he had four Vietnamese lawyers on-hand to dispute and deny any warrant that might await him at the front door.

Strolling in the well-lit backyard to view the waxing moon reflect off the calm Pacific, Billy, Big Man and the lawyers enjoyed a mid-autumn evening as if nothing had happened.

The cocky Vietnamese gang leader was only 34 years old, good looking, well dressed...and tall. *Very* tall, especially for a man from a country not known for producing many basketball players. At six-foot-six, Little Billy towered over the five men surrounding him. Even his bodyguard, Big Man, came in at only five-foot-ten...but *very* muscular and sinister-looking.

Nearing the cliff, Big Man tapped Billy's shoulder and pointed to the right, over the ocean. A Navy helicopter was heading south about a half-mile off the coast.

The bodyguard informed them, "Cho lo su kiem soat, [Just more surveillance,]" as all eyes followed the chopper slowly travel across the tranquil panorama from right to left.

His boss arrogantly exclaimed, "Co mot ngay nao do minh se diet tru nhung thang tu tren troi roi xuong da xia vao chuyen cua chung ta. [We'll soon get to blow one of those nosey bastards out of the sky.]"

The lawyers laughed, though they were hoping their client didn't mean what he said.

Big Man's face showed he wanted nothing more than seeing an American chopper go down. He looked up at Little Billy and offered, "Toi hy vong anh cho toi *danh* du giet nhung thang do. [I hope you'll allow *me* the honor of pulling the trigger.]

Loudly and sarcastically, Billy belted out, "Bon chung toi day tai vi tui no bi tan cong hom nay, suy nghi tui *minh* co nhung tay vao chuyen do ma. [They're likely here because of today's attack, thinking *we* had something to do with it.]"

With the others again laughing at Billy's comment, Big Man loyally decreed, "Day la vu dau tien tui minh tan cong tui no, [Our first blow against them,]" with the chopper now far away.

Trying to lighten the mood, Little Billy interjected, "Hay la tui no toi day de coi *cai nha huy* hoang cua chung da mua cho chung ta. [Or maybe they're here to look at the *beautiful home* they bought for me.]"

While viewing the surveillance helicopter, the men were unaware of the ominous and unlit UH60 Black Hawk Assault Chopper with no markings or numbers about three miles from the coast, seventy-five feet above the water...and heading straight for the cliff.

The well-trained pilot handled the controls like the pro he was. Neither his helmet or flight-suit bore insignias, a rank or name. Rixey was strapped into the co-pilot's seat, with Pai Lee secured into the seat behind them. Each wore flight-suits and helmets. She had no idea what would be happening, but was excited and ready for *anything* as she peered through the windscreen.

About a mile from the bluff, the chopper stopped its forward motion and the pilot spoke into his headset, "Target is directly ahead and at the predetermined distance, sir."

Rixey gave a sly smile, turned to Valentine and asked via his headset, "Ready?"

Getting the thumbs-up, he faced forward and gave the order, "Let's get to work."

The pilot brought the chopper up to two-hundred feet and hovered as he flipped an overhead switch, lowering infrared goggles over his eyes. Flipping a second switch, he watched two thin laser beams emit from a missile turret on each side of the chopper's small wings...pointing directly to the mansion on the bluff.

A house-guard making his normal rounds entered the expansive two-floor living room. It didn't take long to notice a prism of light bathe the room once one of the lasers came through the large window and reflected off the crystals of a chandelier.

Knowing something was wrong, the guard ran out the back door pointing to the house and screaming, "*Coi kia! coi kia! Cai gi vay?* [*Hey! Hey! Look at that! What is it?*]

Little Billy, Big Man and the four lawyers looked at the mansion to see the room flashing colors.

Just as Billy and Big Man realized what was about to happen, the Black Hawk's pilot pressed a button on his stick, firing two small laser-guided missiles toward the cliff. The Vietnamese mobsters turned toward the ocean to see the projectiles rapidly approach, then zoom right over their heads and simultaneously strike where each laser sent them.

The explosions were controlled and not as massive as one would expect…but just enough to quickly turn the mansion and everyone inside into ashes. The concussion knocked those in the backyard to the ground. Once the lawyers were up, they ran toward the road to get away from whatever might happen next.

Billy screamed at the top of his lungs that his *beautiful home* was destroyed and in flames. Big Man helped his boss up, only to see the Black Hawk forty feet above them and close enough for Rixey to view the faces of the two men responsible for his friend-and-comrade's death. He removed his helmet so the two men, with the wind of the blades blowing in their faces, could see him.

Little Billy couldn't believe who it was. Anger brought out his English as he raised his arms and yelled, "*Fuckin' Rixey!*"

Rixey winked at his targets and said, "The missiles were from The Major. *This*…is from me." He moved his hand down-and-to-the-right on the stick between his legs, then pulled the trigger.

Mounted under the right wing, a GE-M134 7.62mm 6-barreled minigun pointed down-and-to-the-right, then fired…washing Little Billy and Big Man in a barrage of lead. Their bodies immediately turned into unidentifiable masses.

The burst of bullets stopped.

The helicopter hovered for a few seconds so Rixey could reconnoiter the situation, then turned and flew over the ocean into the darkness.

Police cars, fire trucks and ambulances were at the scene within four minutes…having been advised in advance of what was going to happen.

Once the UH60 Black Hawk was three miles out, the pilot turned north and headed back to the Point Mugu Naval Base.

Speaking into his headset, with the pilot and Valentine listening, Rixey proudly reported to his superior, "Operation Payback concluded, sir."

Valentine wasn't thrilled to be dealing with Colonel Hartman again, especially when he said, "Good work, Rixey. I knew you'd resolve the situation. And thank *you* for your co-operation and assistance *again*, Agent Valentine." She wanted to *again* interrupt and tell him, "It's *Special Agent*…" but thought twice about it. He continued with, "It will be duly noted."

Unsure *what* to say, she uttered, "Uhm…yes sir. You're welcome, sir."

Barely letting Valentine get her words out, Hartman ended the conversation saying, "I think they got the message, Rix. I'll be there in two days. Put it on your schedule. Out."

And he was gone.

The chopper's propellers were winding down when Rixey and Valentine hopped out. He turned and saluted the pilot, who sharply and officially returned it. Within seconds, a Point Mugu Naval Base SUV arrived with more salutes between Rixey, the driver and a guard.

He stepped aside to let Valentine into the back seat, and joked, "I bet none of your friends at the FBI did anything like this today," with a wink.

She smiled, nodded her head in agreement, then looked at him… differently. She was attracted. But just as quickly, she remembered who paid her and what she was paid to do.

Before getting in the SUV, Valentine quietly ordered, "We have to talk."

He looked at her eyes and asked, "Ever eat at a place called Geoffrey's?"

ANOTHER REMINDER

*"To understand the meaning of one story,
you must often know the details of several others."*

Italian Proverb

CHAPTER 23

There's A Girl In Texas Who Would Like To Thank You

It was too cold to sit outside along Geoffrey's railing, so Rixey and Pai Lee chose a booth inside that provided a view of the ocean. A busboy was clearing their plates and the server slid two cups of coffee and one dessert onto the table. It was evident they were comfortable together as they spoke. But Rixey had to wait for the restaurant employees to depart so only Pai Lee could hear what he was saying.

Once they stepped away, he picked up where they left off.

"So at nineteen, there I was, in the Marines and deployed in August of nineteen-ninety as part of Desert Shield in the first Gulf War. Then it escalated to Desert Storm during January and February. I stayed for the rest of ninety-one to do some clean-up work. By the time we got to Bosnia in ninety-five, certain *government agencies* took notice of particular traits I had and what I stood for."

"Traits?" Pai Lee inquired, without making it sound too official.

"They realized I worked better when it was for something I believe in. *Really* believe in."

"Yeah, I sorta caught that over the last few hours," she threw in with a chuckle.

He grinned and continued, "By late ninety-five, after putting my time in the Bosnia-Herzegovina *intervention*, I was transferred out of the Marines and started doing undercover operations."

"For the NSA?"

He didn't reply and kept going, "Some guys were in it for the espionage. Others were the blood-and-guts type. Me? I was just doing what had to be done. That was it. Plain and simple," then he stopped to laugh at what he was about to say. "Sometimes the missions got a little risky, but I always

managed to come out alive. That was when they gave me my name. Risky…
Rixey. Get it?"

She couldn't help but smile at the story, then hoped to get an answer
when she asked, "What's your *real* name?"

He respectfully shook his head.

She understood and nodded hers back, then took a shot at another one.
"Married?"

"Was."

Seeing a potential reason as to why she was hunting him in the first
place, Valentine announced…but not *too* loud, "So *that's* what your
sideline's all about. She *took you* in a bad divorce." The FBI agent then sat
back, seemingly proud of her detective work.

For the first time that evening, Rixey's eyes moved from his dinner
guest to the ocean, where he stared for a while before revealing, "No. She
died. Several years ago."

A ton of bricks had just landed on Pai Lee's chest. It was the one answer
she didn't expect and could only utter "I'm so sorry" to express her regret
for saying what she did.

"It was Caroline's brother…" he started.

"Sorry…I'm not sure what you're referring to."

Rixey started again.

"It was Caroline's brother who got me into my *sideline*."

"Caroline was your wife?"

"Yeah. After I left the Marines and we were dating, she always wanted
me to do things for people who needed someone on their side. She was
that kind of person. At the time I was doing some domestic and Zone Four
work for the company, so I couldn't--"

Valentine stopped him with, "Zone Four?"

"Asian Operations. My *community*. Anyway, I had money, a nice place
to live and all, yet I couldn't tell her what I was doing. So I went to college,
and with the help of some military and political contacts, I was able to get
right into law school and started planning for our future 'cause I wasn't
planning to keep my company job this long."

"It's nice to have friends in high places, huh?"

He winked and said, "The highest."

"The company? The NSA?"

"We don't really have any letters. Think of it as an invisible branch that takes care of little international problems before they become big worldly ones. Good?"

Accepting what he said, Pai Lee sipped her coffee and spooned away at the dessert they were to share, but she had consumed. She was still stunned at having dinner with the murderer she had been tracking and was now attracted to. She had to shake the thoughts going through her head, so she took it someplace else.

"What was that about the brother?"

He thought for a few seconds before deciding to go on.

"Andy was a good kid. A *real* good kid. My wife loved him. *I* loved him. It was during my college years. He met this girl. She was *beautiful* and he fell hard. *Real* hard. A few months later, she's pregnant. They got married, she had the baby and Andy busted his ass. He worked more hours and bought a house. The best he could afford. They moved in and were happy. Well...at least *he* was." Rixey raised an eyebrow to emphasize his next words of, "Seemed she had *other* plans."

Valentine put both hands on the table, leaned forward and asked, "Why do I feel there's a Spousal Abuse charge waiting around the corner?"

"About a year later, Andy's out with me shopping for his kid's birthday. I dropped him off at home, and about two hours later he's calling us from jail. Caroline and I watched as his wife accused him of assault and threatening her life." Anger enveloped Rixey's face as he continued, "I *knew* this kid. He wouldn't do that. He *couldn't* do that."

Hoping to calm him a bit, Valentine reached across the table and placed her hands on one of his. It was the first time they touched...and it felt good to each of them. It *did* calm him enough to go on after she asked, "*Knew?*"

"He lost it all. His lawyer couldn't do a thing against the charges. They had the kid. Civil and Family Court pretty much consider the male guilty once the mother points a finger and claims she was assaulted or a weapon was involved. After I became an attorney, I found out Andy's judge was on the take for decades. The kid lost the right to see his son. He lost his house. He couldn't think straight, so he lost--"

"Lost his job…and then he lost his mind," Valentine interrupted. "Thanks to *you*, I've heard that story several times recently," then she looked as sad as the man across from her.

Wanting to finish his painful saga, he tried to wrap it up.

"He didn't have a place to live, so we told him to stay with us until he got back on track. A couple of days before Andy arrived, Caroline and I went to the marina to work on our boat. We were going to take him sailing for a few days."

"Where were you living?"

Again, he nonchalantly shook his head. And again, she understood and nodded hers back.

"The boat was dry-docked and going in the water the next day. We were using electric sanders on the hull." Rixey's face turned sullen. "I never heard a thing until the power went off. She was standing in a small puddle and must have dropped the sander. It hit the puddle…she was barefoot…"

"Oh god," was all Pai Lee could whisper and saw how difficult it was for him to say, "By the time I got to her…she was gone.

They stared at each other for a long awkward moment of silence before he again gazed at the ocean so he could go on.

"Andy was devastated. Losing his sister on top of everything else… it was too much for him. Three weeks later he went for a drive. He said he wanted to clear his head." Rixey took another deep breath to complete what he wanted to say. "They said he was going too fast and couldn't make the curve." After a *deeper* breath, he exhaled and said, "Maybe he didn't want to." Gathering himself, he declared with conviction, "*That* was when I chose Divorce Law."

Looking at Valentine to see tears running down her face, Rixey took his napkin, reached across the table and wiped them. He was happy to have found someone he could talk to…as long as she didn't try to arrest him. Feeling comfortable, he went on.

"It was amazing. I watched Domestic Assault charges climb. And the more I looked into them, the more bullshit I found. When I looked on a *national level*…it made me sick." He shook his head in disgust. "And once you throw in a disreputable lawyer or judge, it becomes a one-sided circus. Someone came up with a name for it several years ago. Spousal Abuse Syndrome."

Without taking her eyes from him, she said, "And about a year ago, you decided to start doing something about it."

Not answering, he kept going, "On the whole, most people deal with it. You know, with a divorce. They have family, money, they don't lose their jobs. They mentally handle it and move on. But the ones that couldn't, the ones that were full of love and trust, the ones that were taken by those they trusted and loved the most, people like Andy...I had to do something about it." Holding back his own tears, along with the pain and anger within him, Rixey looked at Pai Lee and softly said, "I stop them from ever doing it again."

She stared at him. She got it. And he saw that she got it.

Knowing that if she ever got the chance to meet her target, there were things Valentine wanted to say to him privately. She figured this was a good time and confided, "After meeting the ex-spouses, learning about them and seeing what devastating things happened to them, don't think for a second I didn't believe your victims got what they deserved." She again reached over, held his hand with both of hers and whispered, "There's a girl in Texas who would like to thank you, I can tell you that."

Peering into her, he asked, "Becky?"

Valentine nodded her head, then attested, "I saw what he put her though. It was a shame. A sickening-fuckin'-shame. I saw the pictures of what you did to him. In a situation like *hers*, even *that* wasn't painful enough for that bastard."

"Trust me. It was," he replied. "The first three were perfectly placed and painful before the fourth one took him out."

Seeing as she had him talking, she tried for a little more.

"Why Asia and not Europe or Canada?"

"Asia's still my zone. I'm cleared to travel under aliases and with a weapon. So if someone moved or vacationed to one of my countries..." Then he drank his luke-warm coffee and changed the direction of the conversation. "Kids. I never hit anyone with kids."

"Yeah," Valentine replied. "I caught that. My boss was right when he said you were a hitter with a conscience. Though I'm not sure if I'm ever gonna be able to tell him that."

Signaling for the check, Rixey told Pai Lee, "There were a lot of lawyers and judges that deserved getting hit, too. But that would've implicated the ex-spouses, and they had *enough* on their plate." Then he looked at the attractive woman entranced by the last twelve hours of being with him and asked, "Now…you wanna arrest me?"

It took her until the server brought the check and for Rixey to hand over a one-hundred dollar bill to cover it before Valentine could think of what to say. But eventually, she did.

"I dug deep into the lives of each victim. I found out the kind of scum they were and how they used the legal system to fuck-over the people who trusted them the most. And the deeper I looked, the more it sickened me to find people like that out there. To be honest, I have to agree with you." She smiled and continued, "It's nice to know you're not one of them."

Rixey leaned forward and gazed romantically into Pai Lee's eyes, and she did the same to him. She knew she should be cuffing him and reading him his rights. But the only cuffing she wanted to do was cuffing him to her bed.

Then, once again she remembered who she was and why she was there.

"But Rixey…" both of them realized it was the first time she used his name. "You can't be judge, jury and executioner. You can't decide who dies…even if they *do* deserve it."

This time, it was Rixey who slid his hands on top of hers. Valentine's heart raced and her face promptly showed she was taken by his touch. She wanted him…and was glad when he replied, "Let's talk about it later."

With the waxing moon high above them, Pai Lee Valentine and Rixey strolled hand-in-hand along the Malibu shoreline.

For no apparent reason, Pai Lee stopped walking, embraced her prey and kissed him.

CHAPTER 24

Any Chance You Can Give Up Killing People?

The moonlight and ocean breeze came through the screen of the living room's open sliding glass door in Pai Lee's eighth floor Marina City Club condo. A couple of candles flickered on the coffee table next to a near-empty bottle of white wine and two empty goblets.

Pandora was set to Pai Lee's "Private Playlist" as Steely Dan's "Don't Take Me Alive" emanated from speakers throughout the rooms.

In the bedroom, Valentine and Rixey were entwined. Noticeable scars in various places were on each of their bodies. Their lovemaking was affectionate, romantic, erotic…and real.

Sleep didn't come until 2:30AM.

Valentine was under the covers, asleep and naked when the phone on the night table rang at 9:09AM…startling her.

But even *more* startling was when she reached to the other side of the bed to find Rixey wasn't there.

She was able to make out her boss's name on the Caller ID. Being a dedicated FBI agent, Pai Lee knew the phone needed to be answered…but was *more* pissed off that her prey was gone.

Sitting up, she hit the speaker button while trying to recall what the last day and night consisted of…then realized she was so wrapped up during those 24 hours, she never called her superior to let him know what happened.

She groggily opened with, "Good morning, sir. How are you today?"

He wasn't in the mood for pleasantries and started right in with, "Valentine! Where the hell have you been? I came back from lunch yesterday and saw the commotion, then Jordan told me what happened. I went to the Security desk and had 'em run footage from the front of the building." He stopped just long enough to get some air in his lungs, then kept going, "Who the fuck were the guys in the SUV and on the sidewalk? Who the fuck were those Asian guys in the van? I saw you kill 'em, then shuffled into a police car. *What the fuck happened?* Why the fuck didn't you report in?"

While he was blasting into her, she noticed Rixey's shirt on the floor, where it had been since she tore it off of him the night before. As Barrett waited for her to answer, Valentine calmed, knowing Rixey wasn't far. If he *was*, he was either shirtless, or into wearing women's blouses.

"*Valentine!*"

Bringing her back to the moment, she was only able to mutter, "Yes?"

"What the fuck's going on with you? Why aren't you in the office and on your case? Do you know I got just got off the phone with some friggin' NSA Colonel saying something about you being part of a special mission with one of their agents yesterday? And they're sending you a commendation! A commendation for *what? What the fuck are you doing with the NSA?* Will you tell me what the fuck's going on? *Do you hear me?*"

Again she was distracted by Rixey entering wearing pants, carrying a tray with toast, coffee, milk, sugar, orange juice and whispering, "Good morning. Is that your boss?"

Her look and smile showed all she could see-and-hear was *him* as she nodded.

"*Valentine!*"

Again returning to her senses, she replied, "Sorry, sir. I just woke up. Let me get some coffee in me. I'll call you back in fifteen minutes."

Rixey gently placed the tray over her lap and sat next to her.

Barrett couldn't believe what she said, as was evident when he yelled, "*What?* I've got media people, plus *my* boss, wantin' to know what your participation was in this shootout...and *you* want *coffee?*"

"If you want coherent answers to all those questions, sir...*yes*," then she hung up and stared into Rixey's eyes.

He chuckled and said, "He sounds pissed."

"He's got some valid points," she chuckled back.

"I'll have Colonel Hartman call again and clear it up."

"You seem to forget I work for the FBI, and for the last two months I've been tracking *you*. Not Secret Agent *you*. Nine Millimeter Killer *you*. You wanna tell me how I'm gonna explain that I caught my killer, and he's the same guy I just blew up a mansion with in the name of national security?"

He didn't have an answer and showed it with a shrug, then joked, "Really? Is that what they call me? The *Nine Millimeter Killer?* That's a little harsh, don't you think?"

"Are you *serious?* You wanna see pictures of your victims?"

Again, he had no answer, so he kept the mood up and asked, "Have you been doing any thinking about everything we've done?"

"From the minute we sat down for dinner," came the amorous reply.

"And?"

She quickly and seriously asked, "Any chance you can give up killing people?"

Just as fast, he returned with, "As soon as you can get 'em to stop screwing people-in-love out of their sanity and everything they own."

This time it was Valentine who didn't have the come-back and gave a shrug, then enjoyed a mouthful of juice and said, "Good point. But, c'mon...get serious. What are we gonna do?"

He took a piece of toast, bit into it and suggested, "I'm not sure. Let's talk about it after I meet with the Colonel tomorrow."

"Do I have an option?"

"I know what *I'm* gonna do. I'm gonna take a shower."

Leaning forward, he kissed her. It was a long time since Valentine started her day like that. She had some *very* heavy thinking to do before returning Barrett's call...and knowing Rixey would be in her shower was even *more* of a distraction.

Making his way into the master bathroom, he closed the door, turned on the water and dropped his pants.

Pai Lee finished Rixey's toast, ended her first mouthful of coffee with an "*Ahhh!*" and reached for the TV remote next to the phone.

Turning to a morning news show, it was only a minute before they went to the coverage of a burning fortress atop the bluff of Point Dume. Her eyes went wide and she turned up the volume. Footage showed firefighters easily and rapidly turn the tidy inferno into wet smoldering ashes as the voice-over reported, "Residents in Malibu's exclusive neighborhood of Point Dume witnessed some expert pyrotechnics and filmmaking last night as a large home slated for demolition was used in the production of a yet-untitled film, believed to be an upcoming Death Wish sequel."

"*What?*" Valentine yelled out.

"What?" came back from the bathroom.

"*Nothing! Later!*" she yelled back, not wanting to miss what was on the screen.

The newscaster continued, "Streets within six blocks of the explosion were blocked off by police about thirty minutes earlier as two special-effects missiles flew over the ocean and beach. That was when the pyrotechnic experts blew up the home…as if the missiles had hit it. Fire trucks and ambulances were immediately on the scene. No one was injured, nor were they ever in danger, according to authorities and effects crews."

"Get the fuck *outta here!* Seriously?"

The newscaster wrapped up the segment with, "Just another night in Malibu! And now, today's weather for the L.A. coast, basin and valley…"

Staring at the TV in disbelief, all she could repeat was, "Get the fuck *outta here!*"

She jumped off the bed and bolted into the bathroom.

"You're not gonna believe what I just saw on the news."

From inside the tiled shower, he threw out, "What? About somebody makin' a movie last night?"

"You son of a bitch! How did you know they were gonna say that?" she asked, startled for the third time that morning.

"Remember while you were driving and I was texting?"

"Yeah?"

Chuckling and answering at the same time, he told her, "Who do you think came up with that? You think they keep me around because I'm cute?"

He waited for an answer. But it didn't come.

The shower door opened and the naked FBI agent stepped inside.

CHAPTER 25

I Want You In Jersey In Four Days

"It was nice of you to fly out here, Colonel," Rixey said, having lunch with Hartman at The Good Neighbor in Studio City, within the shadows of the Universal Sheraton and Hilton.

"Well, I needed to see you, I wanted to be here for The Major's funeral, plus I want to stop by the FBI office to see the footage and talk to this Assistant Special Agent in Charge, Fred Barrett, if you want to join me."

"No thanks. Watching what happened to The Major isn't something I want to see. *Especially* since I can't take it out on Little-Fuckin'-Billy again."

"Noted."

Both men were casually dressed, which was a rare treat for Rixey to see the Colonel that way. Throughout the short meal, they discussed updates on other Zone Four missions, though neither spoke of their fallen friend, his family and the upcoming holidays. It was too painful because both had known The Major for decades.

Once the plates were cleared and only their coffee cups remained, Hartman made sure no one was within earshot, then removed a folder from his briefcase under the chair, handed it to his lunch partner and said, "Until I replace The Major, I'm assigning you to one of his operations."

It didn't matter if Rixey had something else to do. He had just been given a command, and there was only one response he could come back with.

"Yes sir."

Finishing a swallow of coffee, Hartman asked, "And your law practice?"

"I have two active cases. I can either delay them or have someone cover them. Besides…do I have an option?" Rixey asked with a grin.

"No," came the reply with a smile. Then the smile disappeared once the Colonel revealed, "It's the friggin' North Korean crew we've been tracking in New York City."

Knowing the details would be in the Summary Status at the front of the folder, Rixey pulled it out and scanned it as Hartman kept going.

"They're up to something and we want it to end before it starts. Plain and simple. 'Homeland Security' and all that."

"How'd they get in?"

"Damn high-quality bullshit-ID's, South Korean passports, job visas, fingerprints, family references…the works. All thanks to that little power-hungry prick's friend in Moscow."

"Any idea what they're planning?" Rixey asked.

It was something even the Colonel was afraid to think about. After a deep sigh, he quietly answered, "They're holed-up in Brooklyn, which is a longtime Russian Mafia stronghold. It's obvious they're tied together. As far as what they're planning, it depends if Russia or North Korea can get enough into the country, and no agency's been able to track any yet."

"Can't get enough *what?*" pressed Rixey.

With a pissed off look on his face, the Colonel finished with, "Looks like it's going to be nerve gas."

"Fuck."

The Colonel continued, "If it's from the Russians, it's most likely going to be Novichock. They've been playing with that shit since the fucking seventies and used it against the Afghans in the eighties. If it comes from the Koreans, which is what we expect, it's gonna be--"

"VX," Rixey interrupted. "Same stuff Jong-un used to kill his brother a few months ago." Getting angry as he looked over the dossier, he proceeded with, "Do those motherfuckers *really* want to take it to chemical warfare? They *know* the retaliation would be insurmountable. We'd go right into a global-fucking-war."

"Maybe that's what they want," the Colonel nonchalantly said, as if knowing more.

Reading something into Hartman's words, Rixey asked, "Who? Russia or North Korea?"

Finishing his coffee, Hartman lowered the cup, looked Rixey in the eyes and whispered, "Or maybe people within our *own* hacienda who could quietly benefit from something like that." They weren't the words Rixey expected to hear, and Hartman could see it on his face. "Look...just take care of these visitors before they can make *any* kind of mess. We have our people inside ready to make arrests upon completion of your mission."

Signaling for the check, Rixey again responded with the only answer he could give, "Yes sir."

"Oh," the Colonel continued, holding back a smile. "I assigned that friend of yours to work on it with you."

Rixey looked confused.

"The one you brought to Little Billy's house, then had dinner with."

More than a little stunned, Rixey asked, "Why?"

"She's FBI, and technically it's their turf." Then Hartman suggestively grinned, "And seeing as you two have worked together..."

Rixey looked at his superior and suspiciously wondered, "*Dinner?* If he knows about *that*, does he know about the last *two* nights?"

"...it's standard procedure we include the feds on an operation like this, Rix. You know that," Hartman finished...then winked.

Rixey tried, "Isn't there anyone else I can--"

The Colonel quickly cut in as the waitress laid the check on the table, with, "I want you in Jersey in four days."

"Yes sir."

CHAPTER 26

She Knew The Risks That Came With The Job

Valentine sat at her desk most of the day knowing Rixey had been with Colonel Hartman. She stared at the 9 Millimeter Case folders, the pins stuck in the map, the video of Rixey's recurring face...and all she could think about was how to file a report explaining the details to her boss, *his* boss, and everyone else in the FBI.

She also spent a large slice of the last few hours thinking about the shootout, the death of several innocent people and Rixey's friend, but thought nothing of the two men she killed. Inside was a part of her that showed no concern for terminating *anyone* with an intent to kill an innocent person or an agent doing their job. And *that* was what may have put her over the edge for Rixey.

Boarding the Black Hawk, she saw his passion as he avenged his country and comrade...followed by a cover story no one questioned, with the truth known by only her, Rixey, the chopper pilot and Colonel Hartman.

And then there were the last two nights she slept in Rixey's arms.

Pai Lee Valentine hadn't been held like that since the evening before her husband Sean and his eight-man-team left for Alabama to stop a shipment of diverted military weapons and explosives from getting into the hands of The DROOGSS...The Dedicated Royal Order Of God's Swift Sword, a covert group of Christian militias strongly tied to hardcore KKK, Neo-Nazi and Aryan groups, all with tentacles spread throughout 38 of the 50 states, and with high-ranking members ranging from NRA executives to mid-level politicians who protected the regional underground chapters.

Sean's team was to arrest The Royal Order's top echelon staying in the Renaissance Mobile Riverview Plaza Hotel under the guise of the group's annual religious convention, once the freighter docked into Mobile's port filled with what they were waiting for. Another FBI team would board the ship to capture the crew and secure the cargo. Still *another* team would apprehend the four truck drivers waiting for the weapons to be offloaded and then confiscate the tractors. The last team would corral those waiting in the warehouse for their lethal collection.

Once the ship docked, everything moved into action. With split-second timing, each team did exactly as planned. FBI Agents boarded the freighter and secured the contraband-filled containers, then handcuffed the dockworkers and truck drivers. Sean's team quietly arrested the two tall, bald, strong, heavily tattooed and well-armed guards outside the hotel's largest penthouse suite, then stepped inside to capture the nine faction leaders in the midst of celebrating their anticipated cache.

That was when something happened. The exact details could never be confirmed. According to the headset-transmission recordings, the report on file stated, "Each target was being handcuffed and read their Miranda rights. According to autopsy and forensic findings, one of them was wired with, and detonated, C4 explosives. The blast killed everyone in the room, plus additional high ranking Klan and Aryan principals in the adjoining suites. The explosion resulted in the collapse of the hotel's roof directly above them. Human remains found in the suite were minimal. Those collected were identified via DNA testing."

It was *very* hard for Pai Lee to accept and deal with.

But, she knew the risks that came with the job.

At the same time Sean's crew entered the hotel suite, eleven teams of FBI agents raided the homes, offices and churches of politicians and businessmen in nine states, and charged them with everything from treason to murder to funding a terrorist organization.

It was getting close to 4 o'clock and Valentine was looking forward to meeting Rixey in his Beverly Hills Hotel room where she had spent the night before. Knowing they had dinner reservations at The Polo Lounge, she needed to drive to Marina del Rey, get whatever she'd need for the night, plus clothes to wear to The Major's funeral early Friday morning.

That was when Barrett stormed into her office without knocking. It was the first time he ever did so. From the look on his face and the large manila envelope he was waving, she knew it wasn't going to be good.

"You want to explain this?" he bellowed within a second of entering.

Trying to remain calm and hoping his visit would be short, she answered with the best smile she could muster, "Depends. What's in it?"

"I just had to sit with that NSA Colonel for a fuckin' half-hour so he could explain *this!* He said you were part of an operation they pulled off the other night where that house in Point Dume was blown up. Why didn't you *tell me?*" Before she could respond, he removed a letter from the envelope and read, "Special Agent Pai Lee Valentine has been immediately reassigned to assist this agency on a matter of national importance and security." He raised his head and irritably looked at one of his most valued people. "It says you're to cease progress on any cases you're currently working on, and report to their Jersey City office on December fourth. Jesus Christ, Valentine…that's in four fuckin' days!"

Valentine was dumbfounded upon hearing the orders. Her confused mind raced as Barrett tossed the letter and envelope on her desk.

"What the fuck is this about, Pai Lee?" he gruffly asked.

"Not a clue, boss. Honest."

"You *had to* go on that fucking bomb-run? Shit!" In frustration, he pointed to the Delivery Man's image on the screen and reluctantly grumbled, "Guess I'll put Jordan on '*the face*' until you get back. *Shit!*"

She was about to say something, but reconsidered and kept quiet.

After several seconds of tense silence, his attitude changed to fatherly concern as he continued, "Just do what they want, Pai Lee, and get your ass back here." Then he ended the meeting with, "And whatever it is…be careful!"

She replied with the only answer she could.

"Yes sir."

Then he walked out.

Reviewing the letter, Valentine then opened the manila envelope and slid out a commendation embossed with the NSA seal atop it and signed by its director at the bottom. She looked at her walls and wondered where she'd hang it once it was framed.

While Pai Lee was being lambasted by her justifiably confused boss, Rixey lounged on the terrace of his fourth floor room just above the palm trees and overlooking Sunset Blvd. Eyeing the screen of his laptop computer and wearing a set of earplugs, he listened to Paula say, "New Jersey…the Garden State. The third colony to become a state. Birthplace of Frank Sinatra, Bruce Springsteen, Lou Costello and Brooke Shields. Hoboken was home of the first official baseball game. Thomas Edison's laboratories are located in Menlo Park and West Orange. Albert Einstein spent his last fifteen years living in Princeton and died in nineteen-fifty-five. TV shows centered in New Jersey include The Sopranos, Toma, Boardwalk Empire, Jersey Sh--"

"Very funny. Just get me the case I asked for," he laughingly commanded.

The laptop screen flashed from the seal of New Jersey to the heading, "Divorce Hearings For January, 2018."

CHAPTER 27

You *Caught* Me

Day or night, the view of Manhattan's skyline from atop the Palisades escarpment of Weehawken, New Jersey was one of Rixey's favorites. What he didn't know was that Charrito's, the Mexican restaurant on the cliff-side of Boulevard East he and Pai Lee were having dinner in was a favorite of hers.

"What would bring you *here?*" he asked before taking a mouthful of a Margarita.

"I was stationed in Newark for my first few years with the agency. I still have some friends in the area. Whenever I visit, we come here." Then she changed the subject in order to be brought up-to-date on their objective.

Once their flan arrived and the server was out of earshot, Rixey said, "Surveillance reported seven known-North Korean terrorists are holed up in an apartment above a Brighton Beach warehouse with a fair amount of familiar Russian faces going in-and-out. As of this afternoon, there's no sign of the cargo at any port between Boston and Virginia. Nonetheless, they're certainly up to *something*, otherwise this particular crew of Korean radicals wouldn't be in Brooklyn in the first place *and* be protected by the Russian Mafia. The downside is that our moles found out they're planning an attack for New Year's Eve."

Pai Lee looked up from her dessert and quietly-yet-angrily ventured, "Times-Fuckin'-Square."

Rixey didn't need to answer. The dire look on his face showed the seriousness of the situation. That was when he finished his Margarita and paid the check.

Valentine drove the rented dark blue Chevrolet Impala to the Sheraton Lincoln Harbor Hotel on Weehawken's banks of the Hudson River. They had checked into adjoining rooms under aliases…but knew they'd be sleeping in only one for the duration of the mission.

In the back of his mind, Rixey kept reminding himself he had *another* reason to be in New Jersey for Friday, January 12th, but his conversation stayed on the matter-at-hand.

"We can't move until the package is in the country, and it probably won't be until just before they need it." Then he smiled and asked, "You don't have a date for New Year's Eve, do you?"

It was the one question she wasn't ready for, but there was no one she wanted to bring 2018 in with more than Rixey.

Valentine stuttered, "I…I have to get back to my job, Rixey."

Grinning, he said, "Your job? Doing what? Chasing after *me?* You *caught* me! *Now what?*" After a couple of seconds of silence he chuckled and told her, "The government has bigger plans for you, Pai Lee."

That was news to her, so she skeptically asked, "What's *that* mean?"

His response was a wink, then he changed the subject with, "I thought we'd go into the city tomorrow and hit the Natural History Museum. Sound good?"

"Sounds good," was Valentine's starry-eyed reply.

It was a little after 11AM on Tuesday, December 5th.

Neptune Avenue in the Little Odessa area of Brooklyn's Brighton Beach had dirty layers of snow plowed to the curb and potholed puddles of near-frozen murky water by the dozens. A banged-up, grimy, rust-corroded Yellow Cab drove along Neptune, crossed beneath the elevated train stanchions and slowly turned right onto Stillwell Avenue so the vehicle's passengers could view the stand-alone corner warehouse with the apartment above it.

The two casually and warmly dressed occupants in the backseat were quiet. They knew what they were surveilling and kept the conversation with their driver to a minimum, even though he was a New York City undercover detective in the force's Homeland Security Team. Known to his passengers only as "Mike," he informed Rixey and Valentine, "Coney Island Creek is about a hundred-and-fifty feet from the back door of this place."

"Deep enough for a small boat?" Valentine asked.

The response was quick.

"Absolutely."

"How far to the ocean or bay?" she pressed.

"A mile. Maybe a little less."

"Up to the back door, huh?" Rixey muttered, more to himself than as a question. But he got an answer anyway.

"Yes sir," Mike responded as he maneuvered the cab so his passengers could see what was needed to be seen, yet make it appear to anyone watching that he was being cautious of the potholes. "Besides this place, we know of three others the Bravta use for drugs and swag. But *this one's* been busy for the last two weeks. Having Viktor Aleksey active has our department on its toes." After taking a breath, he continued with, "Our Surveillance has a twenty-four-hour team watching five Korean women. They shop in the Korean markets, bring whatever they buy upstairs and stay there for several hours at a time. And they do it in shifts. As crazy as it sounds, they all work as cooks in Korean restaurants. It's obvious there's a crew up there and the women are cooking for them. I *doubt* the Russians want to eat *that much* Korean food."

Sitting between the two steel garage doors were six burly, bald and tattooed men in coats and smoking cigars. The short-yet-familiar barrel of an Uzi stuck out of one of their coats. He knew it...and made no attempt to cover it.

Once the cab was beyond the building and approached the next corner, Mike asked, "You wanna go around again?"

"Nah. Too conspicuous, assuming those guys outside were doing their job," Rixey replied. "We're good with what we saw. Drop us off at Seventy-second and Central Park West."

The driver gave a nod and without hesitation headed the undercover taxi toward Manhattan, then over to the West Side.

After thanking Mike for his help and assuring him it would be duly noted in their report, Rixey and Pai Lee stepped from the cab onto the Central Park-side curb and watched the battered yellow vehicle converge with the midday traffic.

"You know the museum is on Seventy-ninth, right?" she asked.

"Yep."

"Why did you have him drop us off seven blocks away? You think we're being followed?" Valentine jokingly asked.

"I never come into the city without stopping here...and there," he answered.

From the puzzled look on her face, Rixey knew he would have to explain.

"Here," he said, pointing to the plaque affixed to a post that read "Strawberry Fields." Completing his point, he respectfully gazed at the regal structure diagonally across Central Park West and revealed, "And there."

Seeing The Dakota, she immediately got the connection of The Beatles and John Lennon.

"I had no idea you liked them," she offered, followed by a smile of adoration.

He shrugged as if saying, "Of course," then took her hand and walked the path around Strawberry Fields before circling the Imagine mosaic. Crossing the street, the two momentarily stood before the entrance of The Dakota, John Lennon's stately residence, in quiet observance of the slain global icon. During the seven block trek to the American Museum of Natural History, Valentine uncovered more things they had in common. Other than his penchant for killing people who justly deserved to be killed, she was finding it difficult to unearth something about Rixey that she *didn't* admire or couldn't fall in love with.

While Pai Lee was thinking about *that*, Rixey was telling her about Viktor Aleksey.

"He oversees certain terrorist elements of the local Bratva. Bravta means--"

"Brotherhood," Valentine interjected, showing she did her homework. "They called Aleksey *The Gas Man* when he worked with Novichock seven years ago back in Russia. He's *very* Anti-American and that's why they sent him. Aleksey hasn't done anything here yet, but he's high on everyone's radar. Throughout Russia and Eastern Europe, he has a track record of large and small attacks, so far racking-up three-hundred-plus deaths of anyone in opposition to the current regime. There are reports that he was tied in with some North Koreans over the past two years, but no international agency has any real evidence of it. *This…*this is a new chapter, and not a good one." She thought for a couple of seconds and ended it with, "Hopefully we can make it the *last* one."

Rixey responded with a grin and began having the same thoughts Valentine was pondering a moment earlier. He hadn't experienced emotions like that since he met Caroline in the late-1990s…and never thought he would experience them again.

The last two blocks of their walk before entering the museum were spent in thoughtful solitude, though they could feel the other through the hand each never let go.

The sun had set more than an hour before they left the museum at 5:45PM. Finding it to be a comfortable 55 degrees, Pai Lee and Rixey strolled along Central Park toward Midtown, speaking only when they needed to. More than anything, they enjoyed being together.

Reaching Columbus Circle, Pai Lee led him along 8th Avenue to 52nd Street. They made the left, walked halfway up the block and entered Gallagher's Steakhouse, where, unknown to her, Rixey twice had lunch with Colonel Hartman.

"Hope you like their Porterhouse?" he asked as they were led to a table, revealing he had previously eaten there.

"Love 'em," came her reply.

And she did.

Reading from his phone via an encrypted app, Rixey announced, "Here's the confirmation. A freighter called 'Baltic Traveler' departed the northwest Russian port of Menzen yesterday and will be coming out of the Baltic Basin on its way to Cuba. It left Menzen carrying VX gas, which explains why the North Koreans are here. But to have it shipped *from* a Russian port and delivered to a Russian warehouse…this has bigger implications than the public's ever going to know."

"And it's up to us to make sure they never have any idea," Valentine said with pride and dedication.

"So you really enjoy coming here in the cold, huh?" Rixey, wearing an overcoat, asked as they sauntered hand-in-hand along the wooden planks of the famed Seaside Heights boardwalk. It was now Wednesday, December 20th, and the salt in the 46 degree air wafted off the cold, gray Atlantic Ocean. The rides, the games of chance, the food stands and video arcades were closed.

Revealing a little more of herself, Valentine replied, "Yeah. I was never one for crowds. During the summer my parents would bring me here. The flow of people was one thing, but when you're only three or four feet tall at the time, it was terrifying. When I was stationed out of Newark, I'd drive here during the off-season to walk…think. One can do a *lot* of thinking in our business." She stopped walking to kiss him, then got back to business and asked, "How long before the freighter nears U.S. water?"

"Good question," he answered, then texted their query into his phone. "That reminds me…are you going to see any family for the holidays?"

Pai Lee laughed and told him, "Well, my parents are Buddhists, so they have no connection to any Anglo-holidays. But like me, they party their asses off on New Year's. Well, *Chinese* New Year for them." Looking at Rixey inquisitively, she asked, "Why?"

He awkwardly answered, "I'm pretty much the same as your parents, except for the Buddhist part. I just wanted to know if you were going to be around."

Gratefully, his phone buzzed with the answer to their question, ending what had become an uncomfortable moment for him.

He relayed what was on the screen, saying, "The Baltic Traveler is scheduled to make stops in Sweden and Norway before heading to Havana. It will be in international waters, but close enough to the U.S. coast and within off-loading distance sometime on Saturday evening, December thirtieth.

As if working together for years, Valentine took over, "The VX will most likely be offloaded to a smaller boat while they're outside of territorial waters…I'd say right after sunset. I doubt even *they* would be crazy enough to make a drop-off like during the day." She shook her head in anger and continued, "It looks like these guys wanna fuck up my New Year's."

"We've got to come up with something appropriate to ruin whatever they're intending to do. I say we warm up in the car, get back to the hotel and think about a plan." Then he stopped their forward movement and kissed her.

Waking up in each other's arms on the morning of Monday, December 25th, Rixey called Room Service and ordered coffee, then walked to a dresser in the adjoining room, reached into a drawer and emerged holding a wrapped package the size of a small briefcase.

Placing it next to Pai Lee, she sat up with the excitement of a child and tore at the wrapping.

Her eyes lit up when she saw a metal box with a key-card just like his. Unlocking and opening it, Pai Lee reacted just as Rixey hoped. She joyfully admired the 9mm Walther P38, the silencer, ten loaded 8-round magazines, a box of shells and gun-cleaning equipment that were each neatly secured in perfect foam cut-outs.

He told her it was an exact replica of *his* travel-box, in addition to, "It's easier to handle and not as loud as that Glock you carry around, but just as effective."

The happiness on her face was immeasurable.

Placing the box on the floor, Pai Lee looked at Rixey and cooed, "C'meer Santa. This little elf is gonna give *you* something special, *too!*"

"What about Room Service?"

"They'll have to find *their own* elf."

CHAPTER 28

That's What You Get For Trying To Fuck Up My New Year's Eve

It was 4:30 on Saturday afternoon, December 30th, 2017. America was preparing for a New Year's Eve celebration that was still 31½ hours away.

Seventy-three miles east of the New York coast, the sun had just gone below the horizon. The Baltic Traveler cut its massive engines and slowed on the calm water as a 27-foot Chris Craft fishing boat with extra fuel tanks radioed that it was less than a mile from the freighter and once dusk was no longer upon them, it would be ready to take on the cargo of seven 5-foot tall, pressurized canisters. The freighter's Captain relayed that, though they were inside America's 200 mile territorial limit, their radar showed no Coast Guard or American naval vessels for at least 53 miles in any direction.

Seven miles above, an AWAC lazily circled with infrared cameras that kept a close eye on the fishing boat. From the time the freighter left the Baltic Basin and entered the international waters of the North Atlantic via a west-southwest course toward the American territorial boundary, the Baltic Traveler had been monitored by satellites and passing U.S. Navy submarines.

Once the two vessels' stabilizing umbilical was connected, and with the help of the large ship's crane, it took less than 20 minutes for the Chris Craft's crew of six to transfer, secure and hide the canisters. By 5:40PM, amid the ocean's darkness and under a crescent moon, the ships separated.

Over the next eight hours, the six Russians appeared to be just another bunch of guys out for a late-night fishing party as they eventually made their way into the Lower New York Bay and prepared to steer north after passing Coney Island.

It was 1:47AM, Sunday, December 31st.

In New Jersey's Teterboro Airport, twenty-eight miles from Brooklyn's Little Odessa, Valentine's Chevy Impala and a blacked-out Cadillac Escalade with its driver inside and the engine running, were parked in front of a hangar guarded by three armed, battle-ready Marines.

In the nondescript building's Remote Operations Observation Room sat Pai Lee Valentine, Colonel Richard Hartman and two Navy Captains watching monitors that showed live video of the Neptune Avenue warehouse in Brighton Beach, the AWAC's infrared image of the 27-foot Chris Craft from 37,000 feet, and a stationary view from the nose of a black Predator drone attached to the fuselage of a Learjet 70 parked outside.

In the Remote Operations Simulator Room, Rixey was at the controls of a cockpit watching the fishing boat's infrared image. Placing his hands on the flight controls, he was ready to get to work.

He gave the order through his headset, "Hit the road."

"Roger that," replied the Learjet's pilot.

Once its engines started and the jet taxied toward the runway, the attention of those inside went solely to observing the Predator's transmission.

Along with the view from the drone, Rixey kept his eyes on the fishing boat as it began its northern turn, "I'll take it at five miles from the primary."

"Roger that, Rix."

As the boat carrying the deadly gas began its swing east into the Coney Island Creek, a dozen men in the rear of the warehouse waited for the "Go!" command. They were trained to walk to the creek's bank, offload the canisters, then carefully bring them into the warehouse where the seven Koreans would transfer the VX into devices designed to spray hundreds of thousands of New Year revelers at midnight from drones purchased on Amazon. This would coincide with VX gas bombs detonated throughout Manhattan's lengthy and interconnected subway system.

Three years earlier, Viktor Aleksey used fictitious credit cards to reserve a room in each of four hotels that surrounded and faced Times Square so that on December 31, 2017, four Koreans would each control a drone over the unsuspecting masses. The remaining three terrorists would travel underground and strategically place fifteen packages timed to go off at 12:05AM…from the Battery to Harlem, and from the Hudson River to the East River, using the airflow and ventilation of the enclosed subway system to distribute lethal VX nerve gas throughout the entire island.

"Five-point-five miles to primary. Five-point-four. Three. Two. One. Releasing now," the pilot reported.

Rixey immediately replied, "Got it."

The Predator dropped slightly from the jet as its thrusters kicked in and it curved right toward Brighton Beach. The jet veered left to begin its return to Teterboro.

In the simulator, Rixey watched the gauges and digital readouts, not wanting to get there a moment too soon…or too late. He also watched the fishing boat cut its speed as it approached the Cropsey Avenue Bridge, about 450 feet from where the gas would be delivered.

Once the drone was three miles away, Rixey brought the warehouse into view and tapped the "Target" button…programming where he wanted his payload.

As the boat slowly passed beneath the bridge, large spotlights instantly blazed from both banks of the creek and twenty of New York City's Homeland Security Team appeared with M-16's, along with a Hazmat contingent to handle the nerve gas. The boat's crew, blinded and unable to see the number of police, were quick to raise their hands and not put up a fight.

Through his headset Rixey heard what he was waiting for.

"The package is in our care."

Rixey piloted the Predator to 40 feet above the water. At one-hundred yards from the rear of the warehouse, he pressed the simulator's "Fire" button…ejecting two small missiles from the drone and sending them careening toward the cement structure. Then he declared, "That's what you get for trying to fuck up my New Year's Eve."

From her seat in the Observation Room, Valentine chuckled at Rixey's words. The looks of the three men showed they didn't see the humor in it.

Inside the warehouse, one of the Russians read a text that had come through on his cell-phone, "Police have boat. Get out." Just as he was about to shout to the others, the missiles blew through the walls, exploding into waves of fire and shrapnel, killing everyone inside and setting the building ablaze.

The unlit Predator rose into the sky, turned and began its ride back to Teterboro.

In the Observation Room, Valentine let out another small laugh as she thought, "Note to self. He likes playing with missiles." The others, with more serious expressions on their faces, looked at her as she turned the chuckle into a cough in an attempt to cover herself.

It didn't work.

Just as in Malibu, the New York Fire Department happened to have several trucks and a Hazmat unit in the area and had everything under control within minutes.

At the same time Rixey was told the nerve gas was in the NYPD's hands, four teams of FBI agents in four states arrested two Senators, a lobbyist and an international weapons wholesaler who were immediately charged with everything from treason to money laundering to financing a terrorist operation.

Once Rixey landed the Predator, Valentine's voice came through his headset.

"Rix."

"Yeah?"

"Good news and bad news."

Those were words he never enjoyed hearing.

"G'head," he said, expecting the worst.

"The good news is…NYPD confirmed termination of the seven North Koreans. The bad news…Viktor Aleksey wasn't in the building *or* on the boat."

Not happy about her report, Rixey angrily took off the headset and blared, "He's gonna be one pissed off Russian."

There was still 21½ hours before the ball was to drop in Times Square. All would be well. The American people would never know of the danger they were in.

Two hours after "Operation Save New Year's Eve" was completed, and as the Baltic Traveler neared international waters, the crew never saw the four torpedoes that slammed into its starboard side, sinking the ship in minutes and leaving any survivors to fend for themselves in the dark, open waters of the Atlantic. Russian news agencies never mentioned the ship's disappearance or anything of the thirty-three men aboard.

The following morning's New York City newspapers and media outlets briefly mentioned an explosion and fire in a Brighton Beach warehouse that was due to an illegal drug lab run by the Russian Mafia. "Fortunately…" it was reported, "…no one was hurt."

After spending New Year's Eve in each other arms, Rixey and Pai Lee didn't step outside of their hotel room for the following two days.

On Saturday morning, January 6th, 2018, the CIA passed along intel to Colonel Hartman that a high-level Russian informant reported a private airliner had departed Ignatyevo Airport in Blagoveshchensk three hours earlier. Its flight plan listed Brandon Municipal Airport in Manitoba, Canada as the destination. Besides the crew of five, the flight's only four passengers were known-members of Viktor Aleksey's hand-picked Communist hit squad, and in the jet's pressurized cargo hold were three 5-foot canisters of Novichock.

From Manitoba the men would rent a car and follow the canisters hidden in a tractor-trailer hauling paper products. At their leader's command, there would be no phone calls or communications of any kind until they arrived at their final destination. The tractor would cross the Canadian border into North Dakota. On the afternoon of Wednesday, January 10th, they would deliver the gas to another Russian-owned warehouse. This one was on River Road in Fair Lawn, New Jersey…20 miles from Midtown Manhattan.

Rixey was right. Viktor Aleksey was one pissed off Russian.

CHAPTER 29

I Guess I Owe You One, Huh?

On Tuesday afternoon, January 9th, U.S. Army Reconnaissance Team AK6 sent a report from the frozen, desolate Yukon region of Alaska that they found the wreckage of a private Russian Ilyushin Il-62 jet airliner. Local media stated, "…all twenty-seven of the crew and passengers were killed due to extreme weather conditions experienced while on their way to Manitoba. Russian airline officials will review the wreckage once the weather clears."

News reports of the crash never appeared anywhere else.

In reality, the flight had been destroyed at 38,500 feet by a U.S. Navy F-22 Raptor stealth fighter within 84 minutes of Colonel Hoffman being informed by the CIA…and while the lethal Novichock nerve gas was still over American territory.

The Navy pilot, with surgical precision, put a missile into the airliner's fuselage, two into each side of the cargo hold, and a fourth striking and evaporating the cockpit…all within seconds and without the flight crew knowing the Raptor was in the vicinity. At that altitude and region of the world, with the aid of a strong wind blowing from the south, any gas surviving the explosions and flames would dissipate into the stratosphere and not be a threat.

The Reconnaissance Team found debris from the three canisters. None were intact and there were no readings of Novichock residue. They also accounted for what remained of the nine crew and passengers. Russian airline officials had no intention of reviewing the wreckage.

Thanks to Viktor Aleksey's orders for communication silence, he had no idea any of this had happened.

It was lightly snowing on Wednesday afternoon, January 10th.

Waiting along the shoulder, Rixey and Valentine picked up Aleksey's Cadillac Escalade as the anxious terrorist navigated off the George Washington Bridge into Fort Lee, New Jersey. Since leaving his Little Odessa home, the Russian had been followed by five different cars from the NYPD's Homeland Security Team as he passed from one borough into the next before getting to the Hudson River. Having been radioed the details of his vehicle and its exact movements as it crossed the bridge, Valentine had no problem blending in behind and around the big SUV as it cruised along.

"That's funny," she said. "I would have thought he'd have a driver."

"A mob boss without a driver or tinted windows. It's ridiculous. The boss is *always* supposed to sit in the back. There's no accounting for good taste with these guys," Rixey said with a laugh. Getting serious, he continued, "I can't figure out what he was planning to do with the gas."

"Martin Luther King Day is this coming Monday," Valentine offered.

Shaking his head, he said, "It's not a big enough statement. This guy's pissed and he'd want to do something as big as New Year's Eve. He also knows the current administration wouldn't go to war because some crazed Russian terrorist killed a few thousand black people at a rally. If anything, *other* countries would be pissed off. Plus, Novichock is like VX. It's not the kind of stuff you keep around too long. He's planning to get it, use it *quick* and within a fifty mile radius of Fair Lawn. I just wanna know *where*."

"Well, let's see if he'll tell us when we ask him," she sarcastically retorted while following the Escalade onto Route 80 West.

At Valentine's insistence, the NSA let the Newark FBI office raid the Fair Lawn warehouse to arrest the nine Bravta members inside a mere thirty minutes before Aleksey was to arrive. He planned to greet the tractor-trailer, the gas and his comrades from the Motherland.

Turning into the parking lot and seeing his men's cars, everything looked copasetic to *The Gas Man*. That changed when he approached the entrance and saw no one standing guard. He angrily banged on the door to no response and angrily yelled in Russian, "Chert voz'mi [Damn it!]!"

"Hey! Watch your language. This is a family neighborhood," came from the woman standing thirty feet behind him.

He slowly turned. The rage on his face alone would have been enough to scare most people, but not Pai Lee Valentine. Looking at her, Aleksey growled, "Go away, chink cow."

"Hey! Watch your language, asshole. That's my girlfriend you're talkin' to."

The new voice made the Russian turn to his right to see Rixey step from the side of the warehouse. Aleksey realized it was a trap.

"Any chance you want to tell me where you were planning to use the Novichock?" Rixey took the shot at asking. "We have a bet going and it would be nice to know who's right."

"Fuck *you!*" barked the Russian in perfect English as his right hand swiftly reached into his coat to pull out a .45 semi-automatic. Before he could raise and point it, Valentine fired three silent rounds from her new Walther and silencer…right into his chest. As Aleksey dropped his gun and fell to the ground, she looked at Rixey and yelled, "*You're right!* This *is* easier to work with."

Rixey winked and gave a thumbs-up.

Then Valentine made the mistake of walking toward him.

Coming too close to Aleksey's body, he jumped up, grabbed her around the neck from behind with his left hand and raised her pistoled right hand to the side of her head with the other. Putting his finger on the Walther's trigger, he yelled to Rixey, "Who's the asshole *now*, asshole?"

"He's got a vest on. I can feel it." Valentine calmly said to Rixey, who had *his* Walther pointed at the Russian.

"Shut up, *bitch!*" Aleksey screamed as he shoved the silencer's barrel harder against Valentine's head.

With a laugh Rixey told the Russian, "I said watch your language! That's my girlfriend you're talkin' to." With that, he said, "The kick in the balls is from her. *This…*is from me."

The look on the terrorist's face showed he clearly had no idea what Rixey was talking about.

Valentine winked at Rixey as he squeezed the trigger, putting a bullet into Viktor Aleksey's brain. As the big Russian started to fall backward,

Valentine swiped her gun from his limp hand, swiftly turned and aided his fall with a powerful and perfectly aimed kick between his legs.

The pain was evident in his grimace before he hit the ground dead. Rixey *also* twitched when he saw it happen, but kept it to himself. Valentine aimed her pistol at the corpse as her hero came up from behind and asked, "You okay?"

Giving a loving nod, she grinned and cooed back, "I guess I owe you one, huh?"

Standing over the body, the two embraced and kissed.

At 11:15 the next morning, in heavy coats and dressed for the *very* private award presentation they were to attend in 45 minutes with the Governor, the city's Mayor and Colonel Hartman, Rixey and Pai Lee sat on the cold granite steps of Federal Hall at 26 Wall Street in Manhattan's Financial District, and within the shadow of George Washington's massive bronze statue.

Looking up at the first President, Rixey told Pai Lee, "It was erected on these steps in eighteen-eighty-two because that's where he stood when he was inaugurated in seventeen-eight-nine. The building was different back then, but the fact that it was right here..." He drifted off, eventually returning with, "Can you imagine what he'd think if he were here today?" Rixey then shook the thought off as fast as it arrived.

Though his partner listened, she was more interested in the stack of newspapers on her lap. The headlines of The New York Times, The Daily News, The Wall Street Journal and Newsday each had their version of The New York Post's "FBI THWARTED WALL STREET BIO-GAS ATTACK." The awards were in recognition of what the two had done for New York City and America...but no one would ever know about it.

Looking at Valentine, Rixey asked, "Now, wasn't that fun?"

Putting the newspapers aside, Pai Lee leaned toward him, put his head in her hands and showed her affection with her lips amidst the midday passersby.

When they eventually separated and with her face only an inch from his, Pai Lee romantically asked, "Can we go back to L.A. now?"

Because he needed to be in Hackensack the following day, and not wanting her to know about it, he stood and replied, "In a couple of days.

There are a few things we need to take care of first. Paperwork, reports, briefings...maybe you'll want to see some of your FBI friends, 'cause I'm going to be busy tomorrow."

For a reason he couldn't figure out, Pai Lee rose, causing the wind to scatter the newspapers as she kissed him with every ounce of passion she possessed.

He didn't press the issue from there.

At 6:30 the following morning, Room Service delivered their breakfast. Rixey was already showered, shaved and still avoided asking Pai Lee what she had planned for the day...and she didn't offer any evidence of having anything arranged.

As he dropped the towel from his waist and began to put on one of his favorite suits, Pai Lee nonchalantly asked, "Do you need the car?"

"No thanks. I'll get one from the Hertz desk in the lobby."

"Any idea what time you'll be back?" she queried while enjoying his stage of undress.

"I'm thinking sometime mid-afternoon. It shouldn't be later than that. I'll call you as soon as I know."

"Is it anything I can help you with?"

He laughed as he knotted his tie without needing a mirror, and answered, "No thanks. Just some legal business I need to take care of while I'm here. You go and enjoy yourself."

"Well--"

Rixey cut her off, not wanting to appear rude or angry, but wanting the conversation to end. Putting on his shoulder holster and gun, he said, "And don't think about following me." Eventually slipping his overcoat over his suit-jacket, he finished with, "You work for something bigger now...not the FBI."

Like a spoiled child who had just been told she couldn't do something, Pai Lee stabbed a piece of French Toast, put it in her mouth and let out a sad, "Yes...sir."

Rixey kissed her check as she chewed, then turned and left the hotel room feeling guilty he couldn't bring her.

With an inquisitive look on her face Valentine watched him leave, then stabbed another forkful of what remained of breakfast.

She may have fallen head-over-heels for the man...but she was still a cop.

CHAPTER 30

We Took Him For *Everything*…And He Never Knew How

The minute hand of the Roman numeral-bearing clock on the back wall of the Bergen County courtroom clicked to 9:10. Judge Falzone announced, "He gets one more minute."

The room, as usual, was filled with litigants and defendants concerned with their own issues. The Delivery Man, in his suit and overcoat, sat on the defendant's side of the center aisle in the third row, giving him a direct line-of-sight to *The Club*.

Having watched the Meyers-Evans massacre build for 18 months, the Delivery Man knew this was the day it would come to a head. He just wasn't sure when he would pay a visit to the guilty parties. Now conscious of being filmed, he was careful to not look toward the cameras scattered throughout the building. But cameras-or-not, he wasn't going to be deterred from seeing this one through to the end.

Ginger Evans sat next to May Shapiro, her trusted attorney. Both were dressed and coiffed beyond the norm for a court appearance. Behind them sat *The Club*…where Tina anxiously waited for Steve Meyers to enter so she could enjoy glaring at him. Wearing earplugs, Tabitha watched something on her phone…bored and oblivious to her surroundings.

The defendant's table was empty.

In the rear row on the defendant's side, wearing a heavy coat, dark glasses and a scarf over her head was Pai Lee Valentine.

The Delivery Man kept his eyes on the Evans women as they waited for Steve to arrive.

Pai Lee watched *him*…and the proceedings.

When the clock's minute hand clicked again, Shapiro stood and declared, "Your honor, this is an insult to the Court. Seeing as neither the defendant nor his attorney chose to appear..." Holding up a legal document, she continued, "...we're asking that my client receive everything detailed in this Property Settlement, and that a divorce decree be granted by default."

The judge asked, "Miss Shapiro, are you saying Mr. Pollack was properly notified about today's appearance, and neither he nor his client chose to be here?"

"It seems that way, your honor." Shapiro held up postal documents and articulated, "I have the delivery receipts right here, your honor. Each one signed by Irving Pollack."

The bailiff took the receipts from the attorney and brought them to the bench.

Reviewing each for all of two seconds, Falzone struck his gavel to the sound block and proclaimed, "Let the record show that as of today, Friday, January twelfth, two-thousand-eighteen, the marriage between Ginger Evans and Steven Meyers has been terminated in divorce, and due to the non-appearance of the defendant or his attorney, each item listed within the Property Settlement is awarded to the plaintiff by default." The judge raised his head just enough to look at Laura before saying, "Let it *also* be noted the defendant will be responsible for back mortgage payments of the marital residence and the plaintiff's legal fees, due as of this date."

Then he slammed the gavel again.

It was over.

The Delivery Man was stunned.

Valentine, having never witnessed a divorce before, couldn't believe what she had just seen and heard.

May turned to *The Club*, grinning. Laura and Francine, the mother-and-daughter team that could have made the Axis of Evil shit in their pants, congratulated themselves with hugs and cheek kisses. The only thing that could have made Tina happier would have been for Steve to witness what just happened. Tabitha had no idea what was going on around her, being deep into whatever she was watching on her phone.

And Ginger?

Ginger sat at the plaintiff's table staring into an abyss. Sad, empty and knowing she destroyed the man who loved her...had crushed her. But she could tell no one. *Especially* those behind her.

Having attended their Restraining Order hearing, then two Property Settlement hearings that neither Pollack nor Meyers showed up for, and now the divorce, the Delivery Man closely observed *The Club*, astonished at how they worked, moved, connived and acted as one complete being. Months earlier, the Delivery Man looked into the litigious past of Laura and her late husband. They sued anyone and everyone who innocently or accidentally crossed their paths, and always with the help of local and County judges, thanks to Daddy Evans' cash business.

And they *never* lost a lawsuit that they instigated.

Right after Laura gave Falzone a wink, the women gathered themselves and unknowingly made their way past the Delivery Man and Pai Lee Valentine as they excitedly strode through the large oak doors into the hallway.

The Delivery Man rose from his seat and casually followed them out. Not expecting him to depart, Valentine inconspicuously turned away. Having his prey in sight and not expecting to be tailed, the Delivery Man didn't notice his new partner a few feet away.

Outside the courtroom, the Delivery Man found Laura, Francine, Tabitha and a very happy Tina sitting on a bench along the granite wall. He casually sat across from them, took a magazine from his overcoat pocket, held it to his face and started reading…or at least that's what he appeared to be doing. Attaching a pen to the top of the magazine, he tilted it toward the women. The pen was a microphone that transmitted to a small receiver in his left ear.

With a phone to her head as if on a call, Valentine was leaning against the wall about 40 feet away…watching.

May Shapiro and a sullen Ginger Evans stepped from the courtroom. Laura approached them as the Delivery Man turned his magazine in their direction.

"Thanks, May. I *told you* Pollack would play it our way," Laura proudly said, more concerned about her victory than her daughter's feelings and well-being.

Keeping her voice low, Shapiro held back laughter as she told them, "I haven't had a case go this easy since I handled Ginger's *last* divorce."

Equally quiet, though joyous, Laura added, "It helps when you have the same judge. My husband paid Falzone for *years* to take care of things for us. I knew he'd handle this one. All I had to do was ask."

"You know, Nan," Shapiro said, knowing Laura well enough to use her *family name*, "I'm glad you never became an attorney. You're the one person I would've hated to go up against." Checking the time on her phone, she continued, "I have to get back to the office."

Giving air-kisses to Laura, congratulating Ginger and waving to Francine, Tina and Tabitha, May turned to leave…happy to get away from the vile mixture of estrogen. Then Francine called out, "*May!*"

Not wanting the conversation to be yelled through echoing halls, the attorney walked back to Francine. Laughing to himself behind the magazine, the Delivery Man followed her steps with the pen. From a distance, Valentine watched.

When Shapiro was close enough, Francine asked, "You're coming to Tina's party tonight, right?"

Shapiro really didn't want to go, but felt obligated and had no valid reason for backing out, so she replied, "Ah, that's right! Today's her birthday *and* she's leaving for college in a few days." May cordially asked Tina, "How old, honey? Eighteen?"

Tina didn't want to be called "Honey," and was insulted to be considered younger, causing her to snidely answer, "Nineteen," then disrespectfully turned to see what Tabitha was watching.

Noting the young woman's arrogance, May looked at Ginger, who was still standing alone in the middle of the hallway, hid her sarcasm and said, "You must be very proud."

Trying to hide her sadness, Ginger mustered the smallest of smiles and nodded her head.

The attorney turned to Francine and asked, "What time?"

"Seven."

"Good. See you then," Shapiro responded as she walked away, this time faster than before so she couldn't be called back.

Laura walked to her solemn, younger daughter, led her to the bench and put her between Francine and Tina, both basking in their conquest and showing no compassion for the woman who just went through her third divorce.

Tabitha watched the phone and bobbed her head to music.

The Delivery Man listened from behind the magazine.

Valentine continued to watch the circus.

Francine pompously looked at her mother and fiendishly announced, "We took him for *everything*...and he never knew how. *That'll* teach him for wanting respect from one of *us*."

Laura gawked at Ginger, not noticing or caring about her pain, and boasted, "You got it *all*, baby." The old woman then reassured Tina with, "I *told you* to leave everything to Nan. I *told you* I'd make that bastard suffer before you went away." Tapping Tabitha's head, the young girl looked at her grandmother, popped out the earplugs and was told, "Tabitha-honey, I hope this taught you to always trust your Nan, and *never* give up your name, your life or your heart to a man. They're not worth it."

The youngster had no idea why she was recited those words. Not caring that Laura was on a roll, Tabitha shrugged her shoulders, stuck the plugs into her ears and returned to bouncing her head to whatever she was watching and listening to.

Turning back to Francine, Laura finished with, "Pollack was the easiest Jew I ever dealt with. I never saw *anyone* so stupid and afraid...and he couldn't take that cash *fast enough*."

Francine noticed the man in an overcoat with a magazine covering his face sitting across from them.

Laura kept talking.

"You know, me and your father go back to the seventies with Falzone. He--"

"Mom...quiet."

Laura quizzically eyed her daughter, who nodded in the Delivery Man's direction. The matriarch looked down her nose at him...then *the eyebrows* went up. She was giving him *the stare*.

Francine stood and announced, "C'mon, we have to get the house ready for a party."

Tina and Tabitha rose from the bench and, along with Laura and Francine, triumphantly paraded away, except for Ginger, who sorrowfully lagged behind. Her jubilant family didn't notice. The day wasn't about *her*.

The Delivery Man didn't see Valentine walk in the opposite direction as he put away the magazine and pen, awed by the women's successful conspiracy.

The clock inside the courtroom clicked to 9:27.

Unlike the 8th floor riverfront hotel room in which Rixey and Valentine had been comfortably sleeping, several miles away on a major truck road in Jersey City, Steve Meyers, having worn out the welcome of his friend's basement a few weeks earlier, was now in the worst of Tonnelle Avenue's dive motels.

The furnishings were soiled, smelly and worn. The TV barely had reception. The cracked digital clock next to the bed displayed 11:27AM, and the phone was ringing.

Unshaven, unwashed and with his clothes terribly wrinkled, Steve walked from the dirty, rusty bathroom to the bed where he sat to answer the call.

"Hello," he barely had the strength to say.

"Steve, it's Irving. I have…I have some bad news."

Steve took a deep breath. Tears filled his eyes. Having no idea how much worse it could get and not knowing if he could take anymore, he prepared himself for whatever his attorney was about to tell him. Or so he thought.

"Your wife was in court today…a couple of hours ago. I…I didn't know we were supposed to be there. We were never…notified. The judge, he…he granted her a divorce."

Steve's lawyer and supposed-friend waited for a response.

There was silence.

CHAPTER 31

*This...*Is From Me

It was 11:44AM and the mid-January sun hung low in the sky. An ambulance and police car had their emergency lights flashing in the potholed parking lot of Jersey City's cheapest motel. A few residents stood outside while others leaned over the balcony to watch three Paramedics rapidly wheel a stretcher out of a ground floor room.

One Paramedic pushed the stretcher toward the ambulance as the others frantically worked on the barely breathing Steve.

"*Hold on, Steve! Hold on!* You're gonna be okay, just *hold on*," one shouted as they neared the ambulance.

Before lifting and sliding him inside, a Paramedic put a stethoscope to Steve's shirtless chest and listened. Looking at the others, he told them, "He's goin'."

With his last ounce of energy and through heartbroken pain, Steve opened his eyes and strained to ask, "Ginge? Why?" as his eyes rolled back, their lids closed and his body went limp.

The Paramedic pounded on Steve's chest as another opened the portable defibrillator, prepared the paddles and yelled, "*Clear!*"

For Laura, Francine and Tina, the atmosphere in Ginger's townhouse was festive.

In the basement family room, Tabitha was planted on the couch with a large bowl of popcorn next to her. There was a huge HD-TV a mere 8 feet away, yet she still gazed at her phone's screen, wearing earplugs and oblivious to those upstairs preparing for her cousin's party. Over the past year-and-a-half she never noticed the empty spaces on the room's walls formerly occupied by Steve's family photos, expensive artwork and memorabilia.

Upstairs in the master bedroom, the beautifully framed hangings were replaced with works of much lesser quality and talent. Ginger sat on the king-size bed staring at a photo album of her and Steve in Hawaii that she had to keep hidden from *The Club*. Looking at the pictures, it was as if she was in a trance.

The ringing house-phone abruptly returned her to reality. Letting out a massive sigh, she answered it…weakly.

"Hello?"

"Ginger, it's May," not sounding happy. "I'm in my car on the way over. I'll be there in ten minutes or fifteen minutes."

Not up to having a conversation, the sad three-time divorcee struggled to say, "You're going to be early, May. It's not even five-thirty yet."

"That's not it. I just got a call…from Irving Pollack."

A jubilant and euphoric Laura and Tina were at the kitchen counter chopping vegetables and slicing prosciutto with the highest quality of cutlery. After filling several large platters with finger food, the two placed them throughout the dining and living rooms…where pieces of collectible artwork and memorabilia used to be.

Francine had just finished hanging a banner across the living room's bay window that read, "On The Happiest Day Of Tina's Life! Happy 19th Birthday & Good Luck In College! We'll Miss You!"

As the three admired the banner, Ginger slowly approached from the hallway, crying. Holding the 8-inch carving knife she used to slice the Italian meat, Tina heard the sobbing and quickly turned. With the first show of concern for her mother all day, she asked, "*Mom!* What's wrong?"

Laura and Francine watched the tears stream from Ginger's eyes. She found it hard to say the words, but eventually got out, "Steve…had…a heart attack." She lost control and broke down uttering, "He's dead."

Ginger couldn't stop crying as she embraced Tina, who was inwardly thrilled and gave a triumphant smile to her grandmother and aunt behind her mother's back. Each of them sinisterly returned the sentiment.

That was when the doorbell rang.

Holding back her demented glee, Francine told them, "I'll get it," and headed for the foyer.

A blast of cold air hit her upon opening the door. The Delivery Man, still wearing his suit and overcoat, stood holding a dozen brightly colored balloons that said, "Happy Birthday" and "Good Luck!" in his black gloved right hand.

Neither of them saw the dark blue Chevy Impala pulling to the curb.

Smiling at Francine, the Delivery Man asked, "Tina Evans?"

Admiring the balloons, Tina's aunt replied, "No, but I can take them. Who are they from?"

"No idea, ma'am," he replied as he handed them over, making sure she saw the envelope attached to the dangling ribbon. Opening it, she pulled out the card to see nothing written on it.

Confused, she looked at the Delivery Man and was facing the barrel of his silencer as he stepped inside and shut the door. Seeing her expressions of shock and fear, he gently put his index finger to his lips and whispered, "Shhhhhh." Her eyes instantly filled with tears as he continued in a soft, calm voice, "You know what you and your family did to Steve."

Now shaking, Francine began gasping for air and couldn't speak, so he continued, "The balloons are from him. This…is from me."

He pulled the trigger and put a hole in the center of her forehead. Blood sprayed the wall behind her as the balloons left her hand and floated to the ceiling. The heavy woman's weight caused her to drop to the floor with a hard thud.

Hearing voices coming from inside, he quietly stepped into the kitchen and stood against the wall, waiting for whoever would show up next.

Still watching her daughter cry into her granddaughter's arms, Laura asked, "Where's Frank? Who was at the door?"

Using the knife as a pointer, Tina aimed it toward the front of the townhouse.

Laura walked along the hallway leading to the foyer as the Delivery Man, with his gun raised, stood against the kitchen wall near the archway that faced the front door.

As Laura closed in on the foyer, she saw her eldest daughter's body on the floor in a puddle of blood. Instinctively, she screamed, "Frank!" She hurriedly crouched next to the body and, seeing the bullet-hole in the front of her head, began wailing.

The Delivery Man came from behind and with the butt of the Walther whacked her on the back of the skull, causing Laura to fall unconscious atop her dead daughter.

Just before the Delivery Man turned to deal with the others, Tina furiously screamed, "*Nan!*"

The distraction caused him to spin around and be face-to-face with Tina. Intuitively, the 20 year old pushed the carving knife she was still holding through his overcoat and into his left side, just above the hip. Feeling the cut and pain of the blade, the Delivery Man was taken by surprise.

Tina kept hold of the knife which exited his body as he fell backwards onto the kitchen floor, dropping his gun out of reach. Her brows raised in *extreme* Evans tradition. With rage coming from her hate-and-wrath-filled eyes, Tina wanted only to avenge the scene on the foyer floor.

Hearing her daughter scream her grandmother's name, Ginger ran into the kitchen and rushed next to Tina who was standing over the strange man's body. Confused at everything before her, Ginger looked in the foyer to see her sister and mother on the floor lying in blood. In shock, she could only gasp, "Oh my god!"

Tina couldn't see or hear *anything*. Rage for the man she was about to kill encompassed her face. Grasping the knife in both hands, she raised her arms, ready to plunge it *hard* into his chest.

The front door burst open. Within seconds Pai Lee Valentine stepped over the foyer's two bodies, entered the kitchen and with *her* 9mm Walther and silencer drawn, faced Tina.

"Freeze little girl! Don't do it!" Valentine commanded.

A shocked Delivery Man looked at Pai Lee.

Ginger froze. Bracing herself against the kitchen wall to the left her daughter, she was still at a loss as to what was happening and who these two people were.

Tina viciously scowled at Valentine. The young woman's rage was too great. Arching her arms back to increase the momentum, Tina's knife started its plunge.

Three silent blasts from Valentine's pistol hit Tina in the chest with such force that her arms spread wide. As she flew back from her intended victim, the knife in her extended left hand plunged directly into Ginger's heart, through her body and impaled her against the wall.

Tina gazed up at the knife's handle protruding from her mother's chest. It was the last thing she saw as she collapsed and died at Ginger's feet.

Valentine and the Delivery Man watched Ginger gasp her last breath. With her eyes wide-open and blood pouring from the blade through her heart…she died.

Holding his left side, the Delivery Man stood and grabbed his gun as Valentine asked, "Are there more?"

"There should be one, but I haven't seen her," he answered, angry that he let himself be stabbed.

"You need help?" she offered.

Pulling aside his coat and suit-jacket, blood was on his shirt and pants, but the pain had subsided.

"Nah, I'm good."

"Then c'mon," Valentine ordered. "We gotta get outta here." Glancing at Ginger's eyes, she said, "She saw us."

Looking at the impaled mother and divorcée, the Delivery Man said, "She won't be tellin' anybody."

Making their way to the door, Valentine noticed no bullet wounds or blood coming from the old woman and asked, "What about *her?*"

Opening the door, he replied, "Never saw me."

Just as Valentine closed the door behind them and headed to the Impala, Tabitha came up the steps from the basement, still wearing her earplugs, calling, "Mom! Nan! When's everybody coming? *I wanna eat!*"

The youngest Evans ventured into the empty dining and living rooms to find no one in them. Turning around, she walked along the hall to see the scene spread out in the foyer and kitchen.

In shock, she tried to scream…but couldn't.

Laura began to stir, slowly regaining consciousness. Remembering the last thing she saw, she realized she was atop the body of her dead daughter and lying in her blood.

"*Francine!*"

Spinning toward the kitchen, the old woman saw Tina sprawled on her back with three holes in her chest. Above her granddaughter, Ginger remained skewered to the wall…her blood dripping onto the child known to others as *Evil Incarnate*. Standing among them was Tabitha, Laura's witless, sobbing granddaughter.

The old woman screamed and wailed until her voice was raw and she could scream no more.

May Shapiro's Cadillac entered the affluent Apple Hill townhouse development as Valentine's rented Chevy drove in the opposite direction. Each car's occupants paid no mind to the other.

"I guess that makes us even now, huh?" Valentine sarcastically asked.

"I'd say so," he replied with a grin.

"We're gonna have to deal with your rental at some point," she said.

"No need. It's not under any name they can trace. Fuck it. Leave it there."

And they did.

CHAPTER 32

The Love You Take Is Equal To The Love You Make

May's Cadillac pulled into the spot Valentine's Impala occupied a mere 60 seconds earlier.

Braving the cold and despising the obligation of being there, the lawyer grudgingly left the warmth of her Caddie's heated seats and 72 degree interior to walk up the steps. With her fur-lined glove, she put on a happy face and pressed the bell.

Surprised not to hear music or the sound of joyous festivities emanating from inside, she rang the bell again.

This time, instead of revelry she heard sobbing.

Uncontrollable sobbing.

May opened the unlocked door and made the mistake of entering.

The hysteria came from Tabitha as she stood over her catatonic grandmother who was kneeling on the floor surrounded by her family.

Too horrified and shocked to scream, May shivered as she nervously uttered, "Oh...my...god."

Rixey pressed his overcoat against the wound to slow the flow of blood while Valentine followed her phone's GPS and maneuvered the car onto Route 17 South, easily mixing in with scores of cars traveling in the same direction.

Of all the things Rixey thought Pai Lee would have asked, he didn't expect, "So, you let the old woman live?"

He solemnly nodded. Holding back his anger, he said, "From what I learned about her, and what I saw she was capable of, leaving her the way I did...it's *worse* than death."

Valentine pondered his words while Rixey moved the coat to look at the gash, then jokingly observed, "You can tell that kid never stabbed anyone before…it's not that deep. Friggin' amateur. At least she only cut the shirt and not the jacket or pants. I *love* this suit."

"I'd like to hear the story you tell your dry-cleaner," Pai Lee joked back as she took her eyes from the road to look at the cut.

Rixey offhandedly said, "I've had worse."

Valentine let a few silent seconds go by, then threw in, "So have I."

The Chevy cruised through Paramus and continued south. Seeing the approaching New York City skyline, Rixey assumed they were headed to their hotel, so he asked, "We're gonna need a little more than some Band-Aids and peroxide to clean this up. Got any ideas?"

Valentine had her answer at-the-ready with, "My friend Jamie in Secaucus is a doctor, and not too far from the hotel. She'll clean and stitch it without leaving too bad of a scar." Pai Lee winked at him and said, "But as soon as we get you taken care of…you and I have some talking to do. Understand?"

He grinned and replied, "Do I have an option?"

His reply made her smile. She didn't need to answer.

"How about we talk over dinner?" Rixey asked as he turned on the car's satellite radio. Seeing it was tuned to The Beatles channel, he left it there. Leaning back, he asked Pai Lee, "Are there any good places to eat in Secaucus?"

"Not a clue," she offhandedly came back with, then recalled where she heard a voice…*that* voice…ask the same question, but on the other side of the continent and about places to eat in Malibu. The memory brought a warm feeling to her heart. She was also elated about the possibility of talking Rixey out of his vigilante sideline over dinner.

Doing something she wouldn't normally do, Pai Lee increased the radio's volume as the piano played the staccato notes of "The End," followed by the last line of lyrics sung by The Beatles.

Rixey didn't mind hearing the words boom from the speakers. He knew they meant something meaningful to each of them, separately and as a team as they cruised into their new life…together.

"And in the end…
The love you take is equal to the love you make."

THE END

CAST OF CHARACTERS

In Order Of Appearance

Tommy	Sherry Hoffman's boy-toy.
Sherry Hoffman	47 years old. A beautifully sculptured face and body. Loves lilies. Ex-wife of Mark Hoffman.
The Delivery Man	See "Rixey."
Ronald Gladue	49 years old. An air of sleaze about him. Has a penchant for young Asian women and bowling. Anita Gladue's ex-husband.
Judge Mahoney	An Indiana judge who can be bought with a smile.
Charles Adams	"Charlie" to his friends. Loved by everyone except his wife Pamela.
Pamela Adams	Ex-wife of Charles Adams. Likes large trash bags.
Eleanor	Pamela Adams' "Aunt Ellie." A smiling friend of Judge Mahoney.
Rick	Pamela Adams' boyfriend.
Ginger Evans	Early 40s. Mother of Tina. Sister of Francine. Daughter of Laura.
Tina Evans	18 year old. Daughter of Ginger Evans. Has been referred to as "Evil Incarnate."

Laura Evans	Early 70s. Known as "Nan." Mother of Ginger and Francine. Grandmother of Tina and Tabitha. Hates men and anyone who comes between her and her brood.
Francine Evans	Late 40s. Known as "Frank." Her own unhappiness has made her angry at the world. Mother of Tabitha.
Tabitha Evans	17 year old. Daughter of Francine. Likes popcorn, Ren & Stimpy, and is easily bored.
Steve Meyers	45 years old. Husband to Ginger Evans. A twinkle of 'constant youth' in his eyes. He loves his wife.
Kyle	22 years old. Tina Evans' boyfriend. She was 15.
Irving Pollack	Steve Meyers' attorney and longtime friend. Anti-depressant junkie. Can be bought for any amount.
Judge Falzone	Close friend of Laura Evans.
May Shapiro	Ginger Evans' attorney. Friend of the Evans' family.
Lester Jordan	Young, eager FBI Agent in the Serial Homicide Division.
Fred Barrett	56 years old. Black. An FBI Assistant Special Agent in Charge (ASAC) overseeing the Serial Homicide Division.
Pai Lee Valentine	36 years old. Chinese. FBI Special Agent for the Serial Homicide Division.

Gary Pogue	Mid-30s. A Texas good-ol'-boy and mechanic. Becky Pogue's ex-husband.
Paula	A computer voice. A valued, dedicated assistant to The Delivery Man.
Genny Stone	"Mama." Mother to Becky Pogue.
Becky Pogue	26 years old. Once-beautiful ex-wife of Gary Pogue.
Anita Gladue	41 years old. Catatonic ex-wife of Ronald Gladue.
Mark Hoffman	46 years old. Bankrupt ex-husband of Sherry Hoffman.
Sean Valentine	FBI Agent. Deceased husband of Pai Lee Valentine.
Larry Becker	38 years old. Conniving husband of Diane Becker.
Wendy Vaughn	28 years old. Girlfriend of Larry Becker.
Phillip Cascone	Larry Becker's attorney.
Diane Becker	35 years old. Wife of Larry Becker.
Richard Hartman	"The Colonel." NSA official to whom Rixey reports.
Rixey	See "The Delivery Man."
The Major	NSA operative. Longtime friend of Rixey and Colonel Hartman.
Hiep Ton (pron: Hip Tun)	Known as "Little Billy." Leader of the original Phuong Hoang (pron: Fung Whang).

Caroline	Deceased wife of Rixey.
Jack Page	Los Angeles resident. Sued his wife for divorce.
Lai Nguyen (pron: Ly Winn)	Previous leader of the original Phuong Hoang.
Big Man	Little Billy's right-hand man and bodyguard.
Shannon Page	Wife of Jack Page.
Chief Lombardi	Chief of the Los Angeles Police Department.
Mike	Detective for New York City's Homeland Security Team.
Viktor Aleksey	Russian terrorist. Known as "The Gas Man."
Jamie	A doctor. Friend of Pai Lee Valentine.

The Delivery Man's Early Hits

Susan Martino, Alex Barker, Eric Gold, Joseph Blum, Tania Butler, Duane Griffin, Shaunt Romano, Kelly Rubin, Stanley Gose, Valeria Lomax, Theodore Schor.